Levi Hutchins

The Autobiography of Levi Hutchins

Levi Hutchins

The Autobiography of Levi Hutchins

ISBN/EAN: 9783337122713

Printed in Europe, USA, Canada, Australia, Japan

Cover: Foto ©Raphael Reischuk / pixelio.de

More available books at **www.hansebooks.com**

THE

AUTOBIOGRAPHY

OF

LEVI HUTCHINS:

WITH

A PREFACE, NOTES, AND ADDENDA,

BY HIS YOUNGEST SON.

" As sweats are good for a man's body, if a man comes well out of them, so afflictions are good for the soul, if a man comes well out of them." — *John Mason.*

[PRIVATE EDITION.]

CAMBRIDGE:
PRINTED AT THE RIVERSIDE PRESS.
M DCCC LXV.

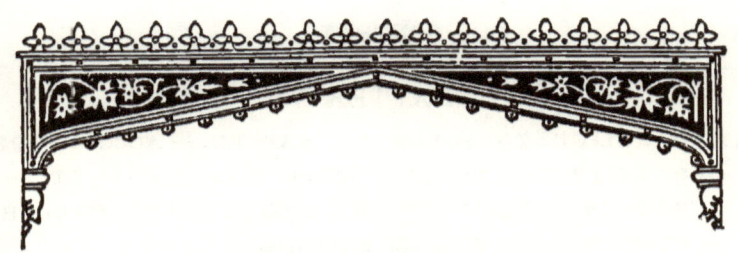

CONTENTS.

	Page
PREFACE, ...	1

CHAPTER I.

INTRODUCTORY, ETC., ... 15

CHAPTER II.

MY FATHER MOVES TO CONCORD, N. H. — COMMENCES STORE-KEEPING. — OUR REVOLUTIONARY SERVICES, EMBRACING MEMORANDA OF VARIOUS INCIDENTS, . 22

CHAPTER III.

THE DEATH OF MY MOTHER. — MY ACADEMICAL CAREER. — FATHER'S AND MY NAUTICAL ADVENTURE. — LIEUTENANT CHARITY LUND AND FAMILY. — FATHER'S SECOND MARRIAGE. — HIS REMOVALS. — BROTHER ABEL'S AND MY APPRENTICESHIP. — SIMON WILLARD. — I ESTABLISH THE CLOCK-MAKING BUSINESS IN CONCORD, MAIN VILLAGE. — JOHN STEVENS, . . . 41

CHAPTER IV.

MARRIAGES, ETC., OF MY BROTHERS ABEL AND EZRA, AND OF MY SISTERS BETHIAH, PAMELIA, AND MATILDA. — BIRTHS, MARRIAGES, ETC., OF MY FATHER'S CHILDREN BY HIS SECOND WIFE, ... 58

CHAPTER V.

DESCRIPTION OF THE MAIN VILLAGE OF CONCORD, N. H. — THE RELIGIOUS DENOMINATION OF FRIENDS. — THE HANNAFORD FAMILY; THEIR BIRTHS, MARRIAGES, ETC., ... 76

CHAPTER VI.

MY MARRIAGE TO PHEBE HANNAFORD. — ACCOUNT OF OUR CHILDREN, THEIR BIRTHS, MARRIAGES, ETC. — OUR CONNECTION WITH THE PRESBYTERIAN CHURCH. — WITH THE SOCIETY OF FRIENDS, . . . 90

CHAPTER VII.

A PARTNERSHIP FORMED BY MY BROTHER ABEL AND ME, IN THE CLOCK-MAKING BUSINESS, IN 1786, AND CONTINUED UNTIL 1807. — MY REMOVAL FROM "THE STREET" TO WEST PARISH VILLAGE. — ACCOUNTS OF PERSONS, PLACES, REAL ESTATE, BUSINESS, AND THINGS PERTAINING TO THIS REMOVAL, ... 120

CHAPTER VIII.

AN ACCOUNT OF MY SON SAMUEL, ETC., . . 134

CHAPTER IX.

AN ACCOUNT OF SOME BUSINESS IN WHICH I ENGAGED, EMBRACING A PARTICULAR NOTICE OF EMBARRASSMENTS WHICH A CERTAIN MAN CAUSED ME. — CHEERING COUNSEL. — AGRICULTURAL PURSUITS. — AN INCIDENT RESPECTING A CLOCK. — LAWYERS, . 148

CHAPTER X.

DEATH OF MY FATHER AND OF HIS WIFE LUCY. — MY WIFE'S LAST ILLNESS AND DEATH. — MEASURES THAT I ADOPTED RELATIVE TO MY PROPERTY. — AN INCIDENT APPERTAINING TO MY BROTHER EZRA. — HIS REMOVALS. — HIS DEATH AND THAT OF HIS WIFE. — MY BROTHER ABEL'S WIFE'S DEATH, SHORTLY FOLLOWED BY HIS. — A FUNERAL DISCOURSE. — CONCLUSION, . . 156

ADDENDA.

ADDITIONAL REMINISCENCES PRINCIPALLY RELATING TO LEVI HUTCHINS, EMBRACING AN ACCOUNT OF HIS DEATH, ... 167

PREFACE.

THIS book was originally designed for a very limited circulation, in manuscript, among my relatives; but several of them having read the MS. copy expressed a desire to see it in print, that it might have a more general family circulation.

Time passes; one generation succeedeth another, and changes in the affairs of human life go on forever. "Look you, the man and the woman have travelled through the round of avocations; the road is becoming somewhat stale and wearisome; it is to be gone over and round again. Must they beat it harder still? See! there comes a little child, a toddling infant, and the man and woman, with this charming puppet for a companion, travel the circle of the year again, and find it all new. They gave life to the child, and the child has returned the gift and rendered them back their youth."

A distinguished man, in his Autobiography, says, "I have ever had a pleasure in obtaining any little anecdotes of my ancestors." Indeed, it is interesting and useful to know the general history of our an-

1

cestors.   One after another of our kindred dies, yet
they live in our memory.

> " There is no flock, however watched and tended,
>   But one dead lamb is there !
> There is no fireside, howsoe'er defended,
>   But has one vacant chair ! "

We recall to mind and cherish in our thoughts
many sentiments we have heard our friends express.
" As lamps fed with sweet oil, cast a sweeter smell
when they are put out, so after death the memory of
persons whom we loved is precious."

Accounts of Births, Marriages, and Deaths, written or printed on paper, are liable to be lost; and
the memory of man is somewhat allied to forgetful-
ness ; hence a knowledge of remote ancestry is often
deficient.   Many documents, which would have
aided me in my genealogical researches, and which
one of my ancestors had carefully preserved, were,
a few years ago, accidentally destroyed.

It is said that " a book should be luminous, but
not voluminous."   The matter contained in this may
be, in some respects, redundant and imperfect, yet
I venture to present it to my friends with these often-
quoted lines : —

> " Go, little book, God send thee good passage,
> And specially let this be thy prayer :
> Unto them all that thee will read or hear,
> Where thou art wrong, after their help to call,
> Thee to correct in any part or all."

From the " History of Rowley," Mass., by Thos.
Gage, and from various town and church records, I

have obtained the principal part of the following information relating to my ancestors.

My great-grandfather William Hutchins' ancestors, and those of his wife, appear to have settled in Rowley (anciently including Bradford, Boxford, and Georgetown) as early as 1639. In 1649 that part of Rowley now called Bradford, was settled. Bradford was incorporated in 1675.

Ezekiel Rogers, a man of great note in England for his zeal, piety, and abilities, brought from that country with him, in December, 1638, about twenty families: EDWARD CARLETON and his family were among the number. Rogers increased his company to sixty families, and with them settled in Rowley, Mass., on the last of April, or first of May, 1639. This Edward Carleton and his wife Ellen's children were: Edward, born Aug. 28, 1639; Mary, born April 2, 1642; Elizabeth, born Jan. 20, 1644. He was made a freeman in 1642. In the following year, he and two other persons were appointed by the freemen of Rowley to survey the town, and register the several lots, &c., of all the inhabitants. He had a house-lot, containing three acres, bounded on the south end by Holmes Street, and on the north side by the Common. He was a Representative of the town, in the General Court, for two years, 1646–7.

The following is an extract from the "Genealogical Dictionary of New England," by James Savage, Esq.: —

"Hutchins, or Hutchings, Enoch, New Hampshire, married, April 5, 1667, Mary Stevenson, perhaps daughter of Thomas of Dover. George, Cambridge, freeman, March, 1638, by his wife Jane, had Joseph, born Dec. 28, 1639; Luke, April 6, 1644; Ann, Sept. 30, 1645; and Abiah, April 3, 1648; perhaps Barbarie Hutson, who, by the Cambridge record, died Feb. 14, 1640, was his daughter, for great latitude in spelling this name is seen therein. John, Newbury, by his wife Frances, had William; Joseph, born Nov. 15, 1640; Benjamin, May 15, 1641, perhaps an error of a year or two; Love, July 16, 1647; Elizabeth, and Samuel; removed to Haverhill, and died, says Coffin, 1674, aged 70. Love married, Dec. 15, 1668, Samuel Sherburne of Hampton. John, Wethersfield, died 1681, leaving Sarah and Ann. Jonathan, Kittery, a youth of 14 years, taken by the Indians, May, 1698. (Mather, Magn., VII. 95.) Joseph, Boston, married, Sept. 1, 1657, Mary, daughter of William Edmunds of Lynn. Joseph, Haverhill, swore fidelity Nov. 28, 1677, was, perhaps, son of John. Nicholas, Lynn, married, April 4, 1666, Elizabeth, daughter of George Farr, had John, born June 3, 1668, and Elizabeth, June 15, 1670. Richard required admission as a freeman Oct. 19, 1638, and so may be thought to have come in the fleet with Winthrop,[1]

[1] The ship Arbella, which contained Winthrop's company, sailed, April 7, 1630, from Yarmouth, England, and arrived at Salem, Mass., after a passage of nine weeks; she was joined in a few days by three vessels which had sailed in her company.

but as we know not of his taking the oath, it is probable that he either died soon, or went home the same year. SAMUEL, Haverhill, perhaps son of John, of the same town, was married at Andover, June 24, 1662, to Hannah Johnson, and was one of the first Representatives under the new charter of 1692.[1] SAMUEL, Kittery, taken by the Indians, May, 1698. WILLIAM,[2] Rowley, 1666, perhaps the eldest son of

---

[1] Mr. Geo. W. Chase, author of the " History of Haverhill," says, that among the laws passed by the General Court of Massachusetts, in 1650, was one against " intolerable excess and bravery in dress." No person, whose estate did not exceed £200, was permitted to wear any gold or silver lace, or buttons, great boots, silk hoods, ribbons, or scarfs, under a penalty of 10s. The wife of John Hutchins of Haverhill was presented to the Court, in 1653, for wearing a *silk hood;* but, upon testimony of her being *brought up above* the ordinary way, was discharged.

From a lengthy account of Births, Marriages, and Deaths, furnished me by the Town Clerk of Haverhill, I extract therefrom as follows: John Hutchins married Frances ——; he died Feb. 6, 1685; she died April 5, 1694; their son Samuel deceased Jan. 18, 1712. William Hutchins married, July 1, 1661, Sarah Hardy; their son William, born Dec. 21, 1662, died in infancy. Joseph Hutchins married, Dec. 29, 1669, Johannah Corliss; their children were: John, born May 5, 1671; Johannah, born Sept. 27, 1673; Frances born June 7, 1676; Mary, born March, 9, 1678; Andrew, born May 22, 1681; Samuel, born Aug. 20, 1682; Joseph, born May 29, 1689. Samuel Hutchins married Hannah Mavrill; they had four children, Samuel, who was born Sept. 17, 1716, Hannah, Nathan, and Abigail.

[2] He was a resident of Rowley from its settlement to the

John, and brother of Samuel, married, Sept. 1, 1657, Mary, daughter of William Edmunds of Lynn, was a freeman, 1682, and perhaps is he who married, April 30, 1685, Elizabeth Growth,[1] who may have been widow of John. Six of this name had, in 1829, been graduates at New England colleges."

From a copy of Births, &c., of the Hutchins family, given in the records of Bradford, from 1671 to 1740 inclusive, I extract the following account of the first three heads of families on the list: —

William Hutchins' children: Sarah, born Sept. 2, 1671; JOHN, born July 23, 1673; Mary, born April 15, 1676.

William and Mary Hutchins' son, Benjamin, born April 11, 1679.

William [2] and Sarah Hutchins' children: Thomas, born Jan. 27, 1681; Samuel, born Jan. 24, 1683.

year 1700. His son Joseph was born Dec. 20, 1666, in that town; and this is the only name of Hutchins on its records of Births.

[1] The records of Bradford contain the following: Married, April 30, 1685, William Hutchins and Elizabeth Growth.

[2] A Council was convened at Bradford, Oct. 31, 1682, for the purpose of advising the people of that town on the subject of the settlement of the ministry among them. The question was referred for decision to a Committee of eighteen persons, who decided in the affirmative. A church was organized there, Dec. 27, 1682, by the signatures of eighteen persons, of whom William Hutchins was one, to a covenant. Jan. 7, 1682, o. s., "Sarah, wife of Brother William Hutchins," was received into this church.

The next account of Births on the list referred to, is the following, and I infer that the WILLIAM mentioned in it was my great-grandfather, whose father may have been the *John*, born July 23, 1673, as before mentioned : —

JOHN and Elizabeth Hutchins' children: Sarah, born Oct. 2, 1694; WILLIAM, born Feb. 22, 1695, o. s.; Margaret, born May 19, 1698; Elizabeth, born Dec. 19, 1702; *Samuel*, born April 10, 1705; Mary, born July 24, 1707; Jérutha, born Sept. 1, 1710; John, born Sept. 1, 1719.

The following is an account of Births in the CARLETON family of Bradford : —

Edward and Elizabeth Carleton's children : Edward, born Feb. 20, 1690, o. s.; Benjamin, born April 23, 1693; Nehemiah, born April 15, 1695.

Thomas and Elizabeth Carleton's children : Thomas, born Oct. 10, 1697; BETHIAH,[1] born March 8, 1699, o. s.; George, born Sept. 26, 1702.

The Bradford records of Marriages contain the following : Jan. 13, 1713, Joseph Sleeper and Sarah Hutchins; June —, 1717, John Kimball and Margaret Hutchins; Feb. 2, 1721, WILLIAM HUTCHINS and BETHIAH CARLETON ; Jan. 12, 1731, o. s., Joshua Warner and Mary Hutchins; Nov. 11, 1736, Joseph Hutchins of Bradford and Sarah Boynton of Rowley.

[1] There is no other record of the birth of a *Bethiah* Carleton made in the Town Records of Bradford till the year 1733.

The Bradford records of Births contain the two following : *Bethiah*, daughter of WILLIAM and BETHIAH[1] Hutchins, born Jan. 9, 1725, o. s.; *Benjamin*, son of the same parents, born Jan. 11, 1727, o. s.

The following are the last records of Births, relating to the Hutchins family, on the Bradford list, (the death of "Davide" being mentioned therein) : —

Samuel[2] and Mary Hutchins' children: Anna,

---

[1] The East Precinct in Bradford was incorporated June 17, 1726 ; its church, of which John Hutchins was a member, was organized June 7, 1727; on July 28 following, fifty-seven women, including Elizabeth, and BETHIAH Hutchins, having been dismissed from the First Church in Bradford, were received into this, the Second.

[2] He may have been the Samuel who was born April 10, 1705, son of John and Elizabeth Hutchins, mentioned in the text; probably his wife's maiden name was Mary Williams, of Wenham, Mass. My suppositions on these points are founded on the information contained in a letter that I received from J. Whitney Hutchins, of Westford, Mass. He says, that his father, Eliakim Hutchins, who died at the age of 69 years, in 1862, had ascertained that his descent was from an ancestor who came from England, settled in Bradford, Mass., and subsequently represented that town in the General Court. He had a son Samuel, who married, and by his wife had a son Samuel, who married Mary Williams, of Wenham, Mass. The names of three of their children, born in Bradford, says Mr. J. W. Hutchins, were Anna, Thomas, and Sarah. In 1740 this Samuel with his family moved to Nottingham, and about four years subsequently to that part of Chelmsford now called Carlisle. They settled on a farm there which has con-

born Feb. 2, 1729; Thomas, born Jan. 31, 1730, o. s.; Sarah, born Oct. 5, 1732; David, born Dec. 19, 1733; Andrew, born June 1, 1735; Eliakim, born Oct. 9, 1736; "Davide diede" Oct. 19, 1736; Frances, born Feb. 25, 1737, o. s.; Mary, born April 28, 1740.

It appears, then, that my great-grandfather, William Hutchins of Bradford, married, Feb. 2, 1721, Bethiah, daughter of Thomas and Elizabeth Carleton, of that town, and that she was a lineal descendant of the Edward and Ellen Carleton, before mentioned. It also appears from Town and Church Records,[1] that some time before 1743, he moved to

tinued in the possession of their descendants, it being now owned by one of them, Abram Hutchins.

[1] The following, relating to the Hutchins family of Harvard, are extracts from a letter, dated at Still River, Dec. 10, 1863, that I received from Rev. John B. Willard: —

"I have examined the Registry of Communicants, Baptisms, Marriages, and Deaths in the Church Records [of Harvard, Mass.] for you. They, the records, are very imperfect; but the results of my inquiries, such as they are, I send you.

"*Admissions to Harvard Church.* — May 29, 1743, Bethiah, wife of William *from Bradford.* Jan. 27, 1760, Lucy, wife of B. Hutchins. June 6, 1762, Jerusha, wife of William, Jr.

"*Baptisms.* — . . . . Feb. 22, 1761, Simon, son of Benjamin and Lucy. Sept. 20, 1761, Esther, daughter of William and Hepzibah. Jan. 17, 1763, Levi, son of Gordon and Dorothy. March 20, 1763, Abel, son of Gordon and Dorothy. Oct. 23, 1763, Sarah, daughter of William, Jr. Dec. 25, 1763, David, son of William. Aug. 4, 1765, John, son of William, Jr. Sept. 1, 1765, Bethiah, daughter of Gordon and Dorothy. May 11, 1766, Mehitable, daughter of William. Feb. 14, 1768, Olive, daughter of William, Jr. . . .

Harvard, Mass., where his wife became a member of Harvard Church, May 29th of that year. In 1744 a *Pew* in the meeting-house in Harvard, "situated by and adjoining the pulpit stairs," was sold by John Martyn, of Bolton, to him.[1]

My great-grandparents, William and Bethiah Hutchins, had seven children, but it is uncertain

"*Marriages.* — Nov. 16, 1752, Oliver Whitney and Abigail Hutchins. July 7, 1756, Moses Whitney and Elizabeth Hutchins. April 5, 1757, Benjamin Hutchins and Lucy Davis.

"*Deaths.* —. . . Oct. 22, 1758, Bethiah, wife of William. Jan. 7, 1761, Ephraim, son of Gordon and Dorothy, aged three years. Sept. 4, 1768, infant of Gordon and Dorothy. March 7, 1772, William, of advanced years. . . .

"May 21, 1750, the Harvard meeting-house was seated, and Joseph Hutchins' name stands first on the front seat below; the position indicating wealth, I suppose."

The following is copied from the Town Records of Births in Harvard : — "Joseph and Sarah Hutchins' children : Lois, born Jan. 22, 1737, o. s.; John, born Nov. 24, 1739 ; Sarah, born Nov. 14, 1741 ; Hollis, born March 2, 1744 ; Daniel, born May 12, 1746 ; Sarah, born July 29, 1750 ; Ann, born June 13, 1752. William and Hepzibah Hutchins' children : Jonathan, born Jan. 26, 1760 ; Esther, born Sept. 10, 1761 ; David, born Nov. 11, 1763 ; Bashemath, born Sept. 7, 1769 ; Eleanor, born Nov. 26, 1771.

[1] About twenty-two years subsequently, the pew was assigned in the mode following : —

"*Harvard, June* 14, 1766.

"For value received of Gordon Hutchins and Oliver Whitney, I, William Hutchins of Harvard, by these presents assign over the within-mentioned Pew to them, for their only proper use and Benefit ; to Have and to Hold the same with all the Privileges thereto belonging, as Witness my Hand,

"WILLIAM HUTCHINS."

whether they were all born in Bradford; an account of them, including the two already mentioned, is as follows: —

1. Bethiah, who was born Jan. 9, 1725, o. s.

2. Benjamin, born Jan. 11, 1727, o. s., married April 5, 1757, in Harvard, Lucy Davis, who became a member of Harvard Church, Jan. 27, 1760; their son Simon, born in that town, Feb. 11, 1761, was baptized Feb. 22 following. Benjamin moved with his family, some time subsequent to 1761, to Putney, Vt.

3. Sarah. She married in Harvard, Dec. 19, 1752, Joseph Atherton,[1] of that town, who died Dec. 5, 1789, aged 60 years; she deceased March 27, 1813, aged 86 years. Their son, David, was born, lived, and died in that part of Harvard known as South Still River. He fell from a tree, in 1805,

[1] Rev. John B. Willard, of Harvard, (his residence being in that part of it called *Still River*,) is their great-grandson. To him I am indebted for valuable information.

Joshua Atherton, of Amherst, N. H., was born at Harvard, in 1737, but I am unable to say what his kindred by birth was to Joseph, mentioned in the text. He graduated at Harvard University, in 1762. He was a law-student of Abel Willard and of James Putnam, and took the oath of an attorney, in 1779. His business became extensive, and he was often the leading counsel in the trial of important cases. He was a member of the Convention for the adoption of the Federal Constitution, and, subsequently, was elected to the House and Senate of New Hampshire. In 1793 he was appointed Attorney-General of that State. He died, April, 1809, in his seventy-third year. The late Hon. Charles G. Atherton, of New Hampshire, was his grandson.

receiving a spinal injury which confined him to his chair till his death. He died about the year 1830, not far from 70 years of age.

4. Abigail. She married, Nov. 28, 1752, Deacon Oliver Whitney, of Harvard, where they dwelt; they had no children.

5. Elizabeth. She married in Harvard, July 7, 1756, Moses Whitney; they moved to Templeton, Mass., where they died some time previous to 1825.

6. GORDON, my grandfather, of whom a particular account is given in this work, was born, according to reliable information I have received, in 1733, at Exeter, N. H., but its Town Records of Births contain nothing in confirmation of the same. He, it is said, was named for a family who lived in Exeter, by the name of Gordon, and who presented the *infant* with a *cradle*, — an indispensable household article in former years. In Harvard, Mass., he married DOLLY or Dorothy STONE;[1] they had

[1] In the records (embracing a period of time from 1732 to 1802) of Births, Marriages, and Deaths, in the Stone family, furnished me by the Town Clerk of Harvard, I do not find this marriage mentioned, nor any account of Dolly's father and mother, *Ephraim* and *Dorothy* Stone. I have referred to her parentage in a subsequent note. See Ch. I. Among the marriages are the following: "Abram Carleton, of Lunenburg, and Eunice Willard, of Harvard, April 30, 1770; Joel Cutting, of Fitchburg, and Eunice Carleton, of Harvard, Feb. 23, 1797. From Dr. J. G. Palfrey's "History of New England," I learn, that in 1633, "three famous divines, Thomas Hooker, *Samuel Stone*, and John Cotton, arrived at Boston from England." The said Samuel went to Newtown, (now Cambridge,)

eleven children; an account of eight of them is as follows: —

1. Ephraim, born Jan. 16, 1758, died Jan. 7, 1761; 2. LEVI, my father, born Aug. 17, 1761, was baptized Jan. 17, 1763; 3. Abel, born March 16, 1763, was baptized on the 20th day following; 4. Bethiah, born Aug. 29, 1765, was baptized Sept. 1, following; 5. Infant, born ——, died Sept. 4, 1768; 6. Ezra, born May 26, 1770; 7. Pamelia, born July 31, 1772; 8. Matilda, born Sept. 11, 1777. The first six were born in Harvard, Mass., and the last two in Concord, N. H.

It is believed by some of Gordon's descendants, that he, when a boy, accompanied his father in one of the expeditions sent against the French in Canada, on account of their "encroachments upon the frontiers of the colonies in America belonging to the English Crown." [1] Gordon used to relate incidents respecting his hardships in going up the Kennebec River to Canada. The account given of him in the "Autobiography," shows that he rendered his country some aid in the achievement of her Independence.

Mass., and was chosen to be a teacher of a church established there.

[1] The rolls that bore the names of the men who went from Rowley, for the reduction of Canada, cannot be found. A Jeremiah Hutchins belonged to a military company of Rowley, that performed duty at Lake George and vicinity, in 1755. I have made efforts to ascertain the names of the men who went from Harvard, in one of these expeditions, but without success.

7. William, Jr. He married Jerusha ——, who became a member of Harvard Church, June 6, 1762. Their children, born and baptized in Harvard, were as follows : 1. Molly, who was born Jan. 4, 1761 ; 2. Sarah, born Oct. 20, 1763, was baptized Oct. 23, following ; 3. John, born Aug. 4, 1765, was baptized Oct. 4, following ; 4. Olive, born ——, was baptized Feb. 14, 1768. He enlisted in the American army of the Revolution, and while stationed somewhere in Vermont, in helping to take care of his fellow-soldiers who were afflicted by the small-pox, died a victim to its ravages.[1] In Saffell's " Records," &c., is the following : " William Hutchins was commissioned Nov. 8, 1776, as Lieutenant in Captain Farwell's Company, of Colonel Joseph Cilley's New Hampshire Regiment."

The foregoing genealogical accounts may, at least, be of some service in aiding my friends who desire to make further inquiries relative thereto. " Were the genealogy of every family preserved, there would probably be no man valued or despised on account of his birth." s. h.

Cambridge, Mass., 1864.

---

[1] The following is a copy of a receipt preserved among his brother Gordon's papers : —

" *Harvard, Feb.* 24, 1766.

" Rece'd of Gordon Hutchins Ten Pound, thirteen & four, in full of all accounts Due from William Hutchins, Jr. Per me, Elias Haskill."

AUTOBIOGRAPHY.

CHAPTER I.

INTRODUCTORY, ETC.

IT has been wisely said, that, " if we have experience, any brother has a right to come to us and say, Put your experience, as a bridge, over that stream which I must cross. I want timber there to walk on." While a man is making preparation for a voyage round the world, he provides things that will enable him to pass through all latitudes, and to successfully encounter a variety of obstacles. I, Levi Hutchins, started on the journey of life ninety-two years ago, and have triumphed over many difficulties that encompassed me as I passed along. My place of residence is now in West Concord, N. H., a village built upon an uneven surface of ground on either side of the main road, over which many wagons, loaded with goods, formerly passed daily to and from Boston. From this another road, in the central part of the village, branches off westward. On the south side of the latter, and about twelve rods from the former, is situated my house. The remains of my wife and of four of our children sleep in the dust. But I am not all alone. My daughter Anna is always at home here; the rest of my surviving children, residing in different places, and also many of our friends, occasionally visit us.

Ephraim[1] Hutchins, my grandfather, and Gordon and Dolly, my father and mother, dwelt in Harvard, Mass., at the time, and for several years before and after, I was born, Aug. 17, 1761. My grandmother[2] died in that town a number of years before this time. Of my grandfather,[3] parents, and five of my brothers and sisters, Abel, Bethiah, Ezra, Pamelia, and Matilda, as well as of other persons, and also of places, &c., I propose to give some account in this narrative or memoir of my life.

My grandfather was a farmer, and also carried on the potash-making business in Harvard. Though a long time has elapsed since I saw him, yet I have not forgotten his venerable appearance, nor all the little

[1] *William*, and not Ephraim, was his grandfather's Christian name, as is evident from what is stated respecting it in the Preface and subsequent notes. This error has been general among Gordon's descendants.

[2] She died in Harvard, Oct. 22, 1758, aged about 59 years and 7 months.

[3] From what I have learned respecting the time of his decease, I infer it to be March 7, 1772. (See *ante*, Harvard Church Records of Deaths.) He was living April 26, 1771, as appears from a receipt of this date contained in a note inserted in this chapter.

incidents that transpired in that town during the
first ten years of my life which I passed there.
Once I saw him perform a ludicrous act, the remembrance of which has often caused me to smile.
For the want at the moment of a more convenient
instrument, he caught up a pair of huge shears,
and with them cut off a portion of his exuberant
beard! One day, in my presence, two young men,
employed by him, threw a live, striped snake into
the boiling contents of a potash-kettle; they seemed
to enjoy the sight of what they had done, but I
regarded their act as shamefully cruel. While at
church, one Sunday, I left our family-pew to sit
with some boys on the stairs; but my father, on
seeing me so situated, shook his head. Noticing his
sign of displeasure at my removal, I resumed my
seat in the pew, but he, thinking I did wrong in
leaving it, corrected me at home.

In his old age, my grandfather's farm and other
business affairs were managed by my father.[1] As

[1] He gave him a bond, showing that "Gordon Hutchins
hath taken a lease of the above-named *William* Hutchins, of
all the Land and Buildings which he is in possession of in
Harvard; . . . to Deliver to the said William Thirty Bushels
of good Indian Corn, at two several times, yearly; . . . Ten
Bushels of Rye, . . . Three Bushels of Wheat, . . . One
Bushel and a half of Beans; . . . to let the said William have
and peaceably enjoy the whole of the South pasture; to keep
one Horse, three Cows, two young cattle, six Sheep; to have
one half of all the Apples and Cider; . . . to have one half
of all the fruit that grows on the trees of his land; and the

2

frugality of habits and simplicity of manners char-
acterized the earlier settlers of New England, it

said Gordon to cut and bring to the house twelve cords of
Wood, and more, if necessary, for the said William. He, the
said Gordon, to find land fit to sow ten quarts of Flax-seed
on, and to pay two thirds of the rates of said farm," &c. This
bond is "dated the first day of April, Anno Domini 1763,
and in the Third year of His Majesty's Reign," &c. It is
signed by Gordon Hutchins, in presence of Oliver Stone and
Israel Taylor.   On the back of it are these words: " A Bond
from Gordon Hutchins to his FATHER."

The two following receipts may not, partly on account of
their *age*, be deemed unworthy of record : —

> " *Harvard, May* 1*st*, 1764.

" Rece'd of Gordon Hutchins, in full of one year's Dowry,
that is mentioned in a Bond, dated April the first, 1763, that
I have against the said Gordon.   I say Rece'd by me,

> " WILLIAM HUTCHINS."

> " *Boston, June* 11, 1767.

" Received of Mr. Gordon Hutchins, *Constable* of Harvard,
for 1766, £33 4*s*., for Mr. Treasurer Gray.

> " Per BENJAMIN GRAY."

The Christian name of this " Mr. Treasurer Gray" was
Harrison.   He was Receiver-General of Massachusetts, and
very exemplary in private life, but accused of being on both
sides in politics, according as he met Whig or *Tory*.   It was
said of him : —

> " What Puritan could ever pray
>   In godlier tones than *Treasurer Gray ;*
>   Or at town-meetings speechifying,
>   Could utter more melodious whine,
>   And shut his eyes, and vent his moan,
>   Like owl afflicted in the sun ? "

Harrison Gray Otis, a distinguished statesman, who died
at Boston, in 1849, aged 84 years, was his grandson.

is not singular that, a century ago, the inhabitants
of Harvard (believing, no doubt, that "silks and
satins, scarlet and velvets put out the kitchen-

In a preceding note, (see page 12,) I made mention of
DOLLY STONE's parentage, &c. From a document in my
possession, I infer that her parents' names were *Ephraim*
and *Dorothy* Stone. On the back of it is written, "Gordon
Hutchins' Bond to his father Stone." It is dated at Harvard,
on the 9th day of June, 1768, signed in presence of Charles
and Israel Taylor, and shows, that " Gordon Hutchins hath
this day Taken possession of the Lands and Buildings of the
above-named Ephraim Stone that he owns in Harvard. . . .
and when the said Ephraim shall think Best to return home
to said farm, he shall have the Privilege of one half of
the dwelling-house . . . during the natural Life of the said
Ephraim and Dorothy Stone, his wife."

In a bill of debt and credit, headed, " Mr. Gordon Hutchins
in account with Joseph Domet," dated at Boston, July 5,
1769, is the following entry : " By half charges upon 16
cwt. 1 qr. 22 lbs. of Potash, made at the Works in Harvard,
belonging to G. Hutchins and J. Domet." By this bill, it
appears, that, subsequently to taking a lease of his father's
farm, Gordon, with Mr. Domet, purchased the said Works of
him, and carried them on in partnership. Not a vestige of
them now remains. They stood on land on the south side of
the road from Still River Village to its depot. The spot is
near some pasture bars and is now marked by a willow-tree.

Gordon's father was probably about 76 years and 2 months
old when he signed the following receipt : —

" *Harvard, April* 26, 1771.

" Received of Gordon Hutchins the full of the Dowry that
was due to me from him, for the last two years.

william Hutchins

fire") did not dress in broadcloths and fine silks. My mother wore, in that town, a dress made of wool and flax, embellished with a checked apron, all spun and woven by herself; and the cloth worn by my father was of her manufacture.[1] Although he had a plenty of room for hens, yet he would not keep them. My brother Abel and I having a great desire to eat some poached eggs, but not having the opportunity, my mother determined to gratify us with an agreeable surprise. Accordingly, she procured a large number of hens' eggs and poached as many of them as we could possibly eat for supper. To "settle" our hearty meal, that we might go comfortably to bed, Abel and I went out of doors and exercised our bodies by wrestling. Soon after this affair, my father provided means for us to ex-

[1] About sixty-five years ago, an account was given of the style of dress, &c., of the people of Tamworth, N. H., assembled at an ordination. "The men," it was said, "looked happy, rugged, and fearless. Their trousers came down to about half-way between the knee and ankle; the coats were mostly short, and of nameless shapes; many wore slouched hats, and many more were shoeless. The women looked ruddy, and as though they loved their husbands. Their clothing was all of domestic manufacture. Every woman had a linen apron, and carried a clean linen handkerchief. Their bonnets!—well, I cannot describe them; I leave them to your imagination."

> Old times are passed, old manners gone,
> And "time is ever on the wing;"
> Old hats and bonnets now are worn,
> And sell for prices they will bring.

ercise ourselves in a more useful manner.   Holding
two new axes in his hands, he thus addressed me : —

"*Levi, I bought these axes for you and your
brother Abel; you being older than he may have the
choice of them.   Both of you are old enough to cut
wood, and I want you to help me in so doing.*"

The axes were nearly alike, and surely we caused
them to cut much wood for the big fireplace in our
house.   But unfortunately I cut my left knee with
mine, and the wound was a long time healing; indeed I have felt, at different times, the effects of
it since the days of my boyhood.   While at our
work, Abel and I wore sheep-skin aprons, this being the common appendage to boys' as well as men's
working dress during my early years in Harvard.

CHAPTER II.

MY FATHER MOVES TO CONCORD, N. H. — COMMENCES
STORE-KEEPING. — OUR REVOLUTIONARY SERVICES, EM-
BRACING MEMORANDA OF VARIOUS INCIDENTS.

IN the summer of 1772, I then being about eleven
years old, my father moved from Harvard,
Mass., to Concord, N. H., where he bought land
and buildings, and commenced store-keeping,[1] in
which business I assisted him, and had an opportunity of seeing and knowing nearly all the inhabitants of the town, among whom was Captain Henry
Lovejoy, one of its first settlers. Our store and
house occupied the ground where is now located
Norris' bakery. In that house, when I was about

[1] It appears by his papers that he had a partner in this
business, for a few months, a number of them being signed

One of their bills of goods was dated at Concord, Sept. 21,
1772. A letter, respecting "Our Method of Trade," dated
at Haverhill, Mass., Nov. 11, 1773, is superscribed, "Mr.
Gordon Hutchins, Merchant, Concord, N. H."

twelve years of age, I had a fever, the first and
only sickness (except a slight attack of the small-
pox which I had in Mendon) that I remember of
having until about four years ago, when I felt the
effects of a paralytic shock.

In regard to the fever, I would observe that the
medicines of doctors were freely given me; water I
was not allowed to drink.   One night, however,
when left alone, I resolved to have some of the
pure fluid of our well, be the consequences what
they might.   Though very weak, I arose, wrapped
some clothes around me, and with some difficulty
arrived at the well, where I obtained water and
drank till my burning thirst was quenched.   Back
I proceeded with redoubled strength to my bed.   I
soon enjoyed the blessing of sleep, and late in the
morning awoke — almost well.   A speedy return
of health was the consequence of thus gratifying
my desire for water.

Immediately after hearing the news of the trag-
ical affair ·which transpired on the 19th of April,
1775, " when the curtain rose on that mighty drama
in the world's history, of which the quiet villages
of Lexington and Concord were the appointed the-
atre," my father repaired to Exeter, N. H., to have
an interview with the Committee of Safety.   The
result was that he received a Captain's Commission.   With much despatch he returned to Concord, and raised and organized a Company of men
who enlisted for six months; but as they were re-

quired to march without delay to Medford, Mass.,
he engaged to supply their families, on *credit*, with
a certain quantity of provisions from his store.   All
preliminary matters being arranged in haste, he, at
my request, gave me leave to accompany him and
his soldiers to Medford, where we arrived in the
early part of May, and remained till the evening
preceding the battle of Bunker Hill.[1]   His Company and two others from Concord and neighboring
towns were in the Regiment commanded by Colonel John Stark.[2]   My father and his Company[3]
were among the number of Americans who fought
against the British in that memorable engagement,

[1] On the evening of the 16th of June, 1775, "a detachment of one thousand Americans was ordered to make an
intrenchment on Bunker's Hill, but by some mistake they
proceeded to Breed's Hill, and by the dawn of day had
thrown up a redoubt eight rods square and four feet high."
The battle, it is well known, was fought on Breed's and not
Bunker's Hill.

[2] He sent him the following request : —

"*Medford, May* 2¹st, 1775.

"CAPT. GORDON HUTCHINS : You are requested to send
a Subaltern and fifteen Men to relieve the Piquet Guard, at
9 o'clock to-morrow morning.   You are first to parade before the New Hampshire Chamber.

"JOHN STARK, *Col.*"

[3] The following were the names of some of the men be-
longing to it: Daniel Livermore, *Ensign ;* Benjamin Abbott,
Sergeant ; Simeon Danforth, *Corporal ;* Michael Flanders,
Drummer ; William Walker, Robert Livingston, Isaac John-
son, Abraham Kimball, Thomas Chandler, Joseph Grace,
Peter Johnston, Samuel Straw, and Ezra Badger.

and in which he was wounded. I desired to go with him into the battle, but he advised me to do otherwise. In compliance with his earnest request, I retired to the highlands of Medford, saw therefrom the burning of Charlestown,[1] and the desperate fight, and although seventy-eight years have elapsed, yet I retain a vivid remembrance of the terrible scene !

Soon after the battle, my father and his Company, including myself, marched to Winter Hill, where he was stationed until the end of the year.[2] On the following day after our arrival there, while we were all sitting on the ground intently convers-

[1] " Charlestown, one of the earliest settlements of the Puritans in New England, a handsome and flourishing village, containing about four hundred houses, built chiefly of wood, was [by the British] enveloped in a blaze of destruction. . . . The conflagration added a horrid grandeur to the interesting scene that was now unfolding to the eyes of a countless multitude of spectators, who, thronging all the heights of Boston and its neighborhood, awaited, with throbbing hearts, the approaching battle."— *Grahame.*

[2] The following Order, Complaint, Receipts, &c., are of some importance as being relics of an early period of the Revolutionary War : —

" *Medford, June* 27, 1775.

" Capt. Gordon Hutchins, Lieut. Thomas McLaughlin, Lieut. Ebene'r Frye, Lieut. Hardy, and Ensign McCary: You together are required to meet at the New Hampshire Chamber, forthwith, upon a Court-Martial to determine upon Complaints exhibited against Thomas Clarke, which, with the prisoner, shall be immediately brought before you. Capt. Hutchins is appointed President.

" JOHN STARK, *Col.*"

ing upon what we had so lately seen and heard, my
father ordered Ensign Livermore out on sentry
duty. He was sitting with his loaded gun across
his lap, and, in rising, took hold of his gun in a
way to cause its discharge, and the bullet was

"*Camp on Winter Hill, Sept. 4th*, 1775.

"To the Honorable Brigadier-General Sulli-
van: Humbly shews your Complainant, Gordon Hutchins,
Capt., That Col. Stark, in whose Regiment I had the honor
of being First Captain, by the last settlement of the Rank of
Officers in the American Army, refuses to allow me my Rank
in said Regiment, and, contrary to the Regulations of Rank
now observed, compels me to take the Fifth Captain's Place:
Therefore your Complainant Prays your Honor would in-
terpose your Authority in behalf of your Complainant, and
order Col. Stark to allow me to take Place according to my
Rank as First Captain, or represent the Treatment I have
met with from said Col. to His Excellency General Washington, or otherwise order or do Herein as to your Honor shall
seem meet; and your Petitioner, as in duty bound, will ever
Pray, &c.   Gordon Hutchins, *Capt.*"

"*Camp on Winter Hill,* 21 *Sept.,* 1775.

"Rece'd of Capt. Gordon Hutchins two Pounds in money,
which is one month's wages.   Per William Darling."

"*Winter Hill,* 19 *Oct.,* 1775.

"Rece'd of Capt. Gordon Hutchins one Pound four shil-
lings in lieu of a Coat for a uniform, Promised by the New
Hampshire Congress.   Per John Gordon."

"Abstract of one month's pay, for Capt. Gordon Hutchins'
Company, in Col. John Stark's Reg't, from the first of October to the first of November, 1775: 1 Captain, £6; 1 Lieut.,
£4; 1 Ensign, £3; 4 Sergeants, at 48*s.*, £9 12*s.*; 4 Corpo-
rals, at 44*s.*, £8 16*s.*; a Drummer and Fifer, at 44*s.*, £4 8*s.*;
42 Privates, at 40*s.*, £84.   Total, £119 16*s.*"

lodged in the body of a soldier by the name of Danforth, of Boscawen, N. H., who soon afterwards died. Poor Danforth, I heard his last moan!

I served under my father as a FIFER from April (1775) to September following, when I enlisted in Captain Lewis' Company, in Colonel Varnum's Regiment, under General Greene. Having entered into this engagement, I obtained leave to make a visit at Concord, N. H., where I sojourned a few days, passing the greater part of the time with my mother. I then went to Cambridge, there joined the Company to which I belonged, and was immediately favored by being taken into the "Captain's Mess," composed of General Greene, Captain Gouge, and other officers. I soon became acquainted with a young fellow-soldier, who was a brother of General Greene's wife. Unluckily, however, my new companion was very much disposed to borrow things without making a punctual return of them. Among other things that he *borrowed* of me was a *ruffled shirt*, and in order to recover the article I was obliged to complain of him to an officer. The shirt was returned to me, but my gay friend left the army.

In the spring of 1776, after the evacuation of Boston, General Washington, anxious for the safety of New York, ordered the greater part of the American Army to march there; to which place he also repaired, arriving there a few days in advance of the divisions of the army. The Company to

which I belonged composed a part of these troops.
General Washington, anticipating that the enemy
under General Howe intended to reach New York
across Long Island, had the precaution to post a
body of troops at Brooklyn; here I was stationed
for a while. During this time, my fellow-soldiers
and I desired to obtain something to eat besides
the salt provisions supplied by Government. With
this end in view, we went one day to a pond near
by, and obtained from it a quantity of clams and
oysters. It proved, however, that they were private property, and had been planted in a cove.
The owner, seeing us in the act of appropriating
his property to our use, made a complaint against
us. On returning to our quarters with our booty,
we were arrested by police officers, who compelled
us to carry it back. Having obeyed the command,
we were sent for a short time to the guard-house,
which ended the whole matter. This was the only
punishment I received while with the army; but
truth compels me to add, that my comrades and I
often helped ourselves to musk and water-melons
that grew in profusion on patches of ground in
Brooklyn.

At length our Regiment was posted at Red
Hook,[1] where we remained until after the defeat

[1] An American officer, Lieutenant Samuel Shaw, wrote
(June 11, 1776) to his father as follows: —

. . . "I am now stationed at Red Hook, about four miles
from New York. It is an island, situated in such a manner

of the Americans in the battle of Long Island.[1]   I saw the flashes and heard the reports of the guns all the time the battle lasted, and was as desirous to be engaged in this battle as in that of Bunker Hill ; but one cause kept me out of the latter, and another removed me from the former.   Although our troops were defeated on Long Island, yet they accomplished a famous retreat therefrom across East River, in boats, to New York, where they landed early in the morning of August 30th, 1776.   Formerly it was rather dangerous to cross this river in boats from New York to Brooklyn.[2]   It is now a

as to command the entrance of the harbor entirely, where we have a fort with four eighteen-pounders, to fire *en barbette*, that is, over the top of the works, which is vastly better than firing through embrasures, as we can bring all our guns to bear on the same object at once.   The fort is named *Defiance*.   Should the enemy's fleet make an attempt, they will, I think, be annoyed by it exceedingly.   It is thought to be one of the most important posts we have." . . .

[1] The number of our troops engaged in the action, inexperienced in military service as most of them were, was only five thousand.   They were opposed by troops well disciplined and numbering three times as many.

[2] It appears from an authentic account of the New York Ferries, lately published in the New York " Sunday Times," that, in 1652, a ferry from that city to *Breukelen* was established by private individuals, and, in 1684, this ferry-right came into the possession of the city.   " There were then no accommodations, such as ferry-houses, &c., and the boats were oar-barges for foot-passengers, and sprit-sail boats for horses and carriages.   The passage across the East River, at that day, was frequently more formidable than is now a voyage to

pleasant *trip* in a steamboat between the two cities.
I have been in New York twice within the last ten
years, and at both times saw some things that reminded me of the days I passed there when about
fifteen years old. The city, which in 1776 had
22,000 inhabitants, now has a population of over
800,000. I have also visited Cambridge, Mass., often, of late years, and each time have seen the now
renowned ELM-TREE, and the house[1] which was once
occupied as General Washington's head-quarters.

Europe. The river between the New York and Long Island
shores was then much wider than it is now. The practice of
docking out has been carried to such an extent, on both sides,
that the width of the stream is reduced about one third." In
1699, a new brick ferry-house was erected on the Long Island
side, two stories in height. In 1717, two ferries were established. In 1754, the old ferries were broken up and three
new ones established, the leases being sold separately and to
different parties. In 1814, a horse-boat was put upon the
ferry, and afterwards, in the same year, the first steamboat.
In consequence of the expense of steam navigation, horse-
boats were again introduced on this ferry, but, in 1824, the
way was opened for the use of steamboats again.

[1] It is one of two large houses built, some time before 1747,
by Colonel John Vassal, of French origin, whose ancestors
were among the original patentees of Massachusetts. The
estates of the Vassal family were confiscated and became
successively the residence of Andrew Cragie, Esq., and of
his relict, the late Madam Cragie, of Joseph E. Worcester,
LL. D., the lexicographer, and, lastly, the home of the poet
Longfellow, who, in his " Hyperion, a Romance," says : —

" It is no longer day. Through the trees rises the red moon,
and the stars are scarcely seen. In the vast shadow of night,
the coolness and the dews descend. I sit at the open window

The year for which I enlisted was near its close. My father arrived in New York, Sept. 2, 1776, (which was the third day of the occupation of the city by the American troops,) from a business visit at Philadelphia, and, after conversing with me a while, inquired whether I would like to go home? I readily answered, "Yes!" for although the turmoil and changing incidents of war comported with my disposition, yet the desire to see my mother preponderated over all inducements to remain where I was. Accordingly I asked for my discharge; the officer to whom I applied urged me to accept an Ensign's commission, and remain in the army. I was pleased with the offer, but said, "Having fulfilled my engagement in the service, I wish now to take a recess before I enlist again." I received an honorable discharge, and had a pleasant parting interview with my fellow-soldiers. Meantime, my father sought for and obtained a young man to supply my place; he also purchased a horse, and we rode home together on the animal's back. Nowadays, this mode of travelling would hardly suit

to enjoy them, and hear only the voice of the summer wind. Like black hulks, the shadows of the great trees ride at anchor on the billowy sea of grass. I cannot see the red and blue flowers, but I know that they are there. Far away in the meadow gleams the silver Charles. The tramp of horses' hoofs sounds from the wooden bridge. Then all is still, save the continuous wind of the summer night. Sometimes I know not if it be the wind or the sound of the neighboring sea. The village clock strikes; and I feel that I am not alone."

people, who go in railroad cars from New York to Concord, N. H. Formerly ladies and gentlemen, while going from New York to Philadelphia, rode in a *wagon* from Amboy to Bordentown.

It was indeed pleasant to enjoy again the comforts of HOME. But, alas! I carried there some disagreeable mementos of a soldier's life, — a number of little noxious animals, pests of the camp; but my mother soon destroyed them, not in the way, however, that an old lady, who lived in Morristown, N. J., in 1778, adopted. At that time, American soldiers, half famished with hunger, often visited at her house; she gave them food in abundance, and to rid them of vermin *baked their clothes in an oven.*

In 1776, my father was raised to the rank of Lieutenant-Colonel in Colonel Nahum Baldwin's Regiment, with which he marched through Connecticut to join the Continental Army in New York. During the march many of the soldiers were seized with sickness, but as no medicines had been provided by Government, he procured some for them at his own expense. About five months after performing this kind act, he petitioned the General Assembly of New Hampshire, to repay him the money for these medicines, stating in his petition that he had purchased them out of " pity and humanity towards the unhappy sufferers, and also actuated from zeal for the public service." Accordingly, he was paid out of the Treasury of New Hampshire £3 6s. 6d.

My father fought in the battle of White Plains,[1] which took place between the American and British troops, on the 28th day of October, 1776.

[1] The two following paragraphs are extracts relating to this battle, from two letters of Lieutenant Shaw, both of which he wrote to his father from White Plains, one two days before, the other three days after, the battle: —

"We shall remain at this place till we have a brush with the enemy. They are within three miles of us. Their movements have been such as to occasion us a great deal of trouble, and it is happy for us that they did not effect our ruin. . . . We have constantly beaten the enemy, in several skirmishes." . . .

"On Monday the enemy appeared in sight, keeping on as though they intended to carry all before them. Our troops were prepared to receive them, when, instead of making a general attack, as was expected, Howe marched the larger part of his army to the right, where we had a brigade advantageously posted on the hill, which commanded our camp. He carried it, being seven or eight times superior in numbers to our party there, before we could reinforce it. Deserters say the enemy had four hundred killed and wounded; on our part about one hundred and thirty." . . .

There are many documents preserved among my grandfather's (Colonel Gordon Hutchins') papers, that I intended to print in an Appendix to this work, instead of inserting them as *notes*, on account of their little importance. Of this kind are the four following: —

"*Camp at North Castle*, *Dec. 1st*, 1776.

"The troops at this post, belonging to Col. Baldwin's Reg't of New Hampshire, now under the immediate command of Lieut.-Col. Gordon Hutchins, having honorably served the full time they engaged for, are discharged from further service in the Army. With the thanks of General Spencer and by his Order.　　Wm. Peck, *Aid-de-Camp*."

At a parish meeting[1] held in Concord, N. H., on the 4th of March, 1777, " Col. Gordon Hutchins

" *Concord, N. H., Dec.* 18*th*, 1776.

" To ALL PERSONS WHOM IT MAY CONCERN : Permit the Bearer, Col. Gordon Hutchins, to Pass and repass in any of the United States of America, and to purchase Two Hundred Sheep, and bring them to the State of New Hampshire.

" TIMOTHY WALKER, JR.,
RICHARD HERBERT,
THOMAS STICKNEY,
" *Committee of Correspondence and*
" *Inspection for Concord, N. H.*"

" *State of New Hampshire, June* 7*th*, 1777.

" To COL. GORDON HUTCHINS : Pursuant to a Vote of Council and Assembly, you are hereby appointed to proceed immediately to Newbury, or Boxford, or any other place in the vicinity of those towns, in the State of Massachusetts Bay, in order to apprehend Col. Asa Porter, if he can be found there, he having lately made his escape from Justice in this State. And you are directed to apply to some Magistrate, in that State, to procure a Warrant and an Officer to seize and bring him to the Line dividing the States; from whence you are hereby authorized to receive and bring him to Exeter, there to wait the Order of the General Assembly concerning him.   M. WEARE, *President.*"

" *Exeter, June ye* 16*th*, 1777.

" Received of Col. Gordon Hutchins, of Concord, three five pound State Notes, being part of the Bounty of Hezekiah Swain, a Soldier in Capt. Livermore's Company in the Continental Army, which Note said Hutchins rece'd of Ens. Nathan Hoit to deliver to me.   Per EBENEZER SMITH."

[1] Among other votes passed were the following : —
" *Voted,* That the Committee of Safety be directed to instruct Col. Gordon Hutchins to apply to the Courts of Judi-

was chosen Representative to the Provincial Congress held at Exeter."

It was fortunate for our country that General Stark was victorious over the British troops in the battle of Bennington.[1] Before stating the particulars of what my father did in relation to this battle, it may not be out of place to say, that the territory now known by the name of Concord, N. H., was

cature of this State, to dismiss Peter Green, Esq., from all business henceforth and forever.

" *Voted*, That the Committee of Safety be directed to instruct Col. Gordon Hutchins to apply to Capt. Parker, the Sheriff for the County of Rockingham, to dismiss Mr. Jacob Green from the office of Deputy Sheriff."

[1] In July, 1777, General Burgoyne invested and took Ticonderoga, and, soon after destroying the American flotilla on Lake George, marched his army to Fort Edward, but had to encounter in reaching it the *obstacles*, consisting of prostrate trees, &c., that General Schuyler's army placed in his way. In the early part of the following month, a detachment of General Burgoyne's army, under Colonel Baum, was sent to Bennington to seize some military stores; but the Colonel, on arriving near that place, was surprised on being informed that American troops were intrenched there; consequently he despatched a messenger to General Burgoyne for a reinforcement. Finally, the famous battle of Bennington, fought on the 16th of August, 1777, between Colonel Baum, commanding the British forces on the one side, and the American troops consisting of a party of Vermont " Green Mountain Boys," and a detachment of New Hampshire militia, under General Stark, on the other, resulted in the death of Colonel Baum and a total defeat of his forces. The loss of the British was about seven hundred in killed and wounded; that of the Americans about one hundred.

called Pennacook, until about the close of 1733, when the name of Rumford was given to it. Thirty-two years afterward Concord became its name, to which was prefixed "City of," in 1853, by the adoption of a city charter. In 1727 a block-house, 40 feet by 25, was erected in Pennacook for the purposes of a fort and meeting-house. About three years subsequently, Rev. Timothy Walker was settled as minister, and twenty-one years from the time of his settlement, he had a new meeting-house built of white-oak timber, two stories high, with its seats ranged on either side of a broad aisle. Within this good edifice he was preaching one Sunday afternoon, a short time previous to the battle of Bennington, when my father, having ridden with great speed on horseback from Exeter,[1] entered and walked up the broad aisle near to the pulpit. The minister, though earnestly engaged in the delivery of his sermon, noticed that he appeared to come into the house of worship on extraordinary business, and inquired : —

"Is Colonel Hutchins the bearer of any message?"

"Yes!" he replied, and added with much ani-

---

1 "As soon as it was decided [in the Provincial Congress held at Exeter] to raise volunteer companies, Col. Hutchins mounted his horse, and, travelling all night with all possible haste, reached Concord on Sabbath afternoon, from Exeter. Col. Hutchins was Representative from Concord."— *History of Concord*, by Nathaniel Bouton, D. D.

mation, the eyes of all present being directed towards him, " *General Burgoyne with his army is on his march to Albany!* General Stark has offered to take the command of the New Hampshire men ; AND IF WE ALL TURN OUT WE CAN CUT OFF BURGOYNE'S MARCH ! "

" My hearers," said the preacher, "those of you who are willing to go had better leave at once."

The men forthwith left the meeting-house and showed their readiness to serve their country by promptly enlisting in her cause. A Company was ready to march on the following morning. Another Company from Concord, under my father's command, marched to Bennington, but did not arrive there in season to engage in the battle.[1]

---

[1] On the 17th of September, thirty-two days after the battle of Bennington, General Burgoyne and his army encountered in their advance upon Saratoga and Stillwater, the American troops, commanded by General Gates, and a skirmish ensued. Two days afterward there was another indecisive action between the two armies, and on the 7th of October following, the battle of Saratoga was fought, resulting in the surrender of General Burgoyne and his army of five thousand seven hundred effective men as prisoners of war. " The whole British Army has laid down arms at Saratoga; our sons, full of vigor and courage, expect your orders," &c., were the happy tidings of General Gates despatched to Congress, immediately after the victory.

In regard to the " obstacles," previously referred to, Frederic Reynolds wrote the following lines : —

 " Burgoyne, alas ! not seeing future fates,
  Could cut his way thro' *woods* but not thro' GATES."

Soon after the battle of Lexington, as before stated, my father raised and organized a Company of men and supplied their families, *on credit*, with provisions from his store. He realized, however, but a small return in payment for these, mainly on account of a *depreciation* in the currency. When the paper dollar passed at a reasonable value, my father sold his store, dwelling-house, a lot of land and a cow to Robert Harris, of Concord, N. H.; but when payment became due, Harris availed himself of the advantage that the law[1] gave a debtor, and my father did not receive money enough for the whole property to pay for that part of it included in the house.[2]

[1] In some of the States depreciated bills of credit " were made a tender for the interest, but not for the principal, of former debts; in New Hampshire if the creditor should refuse them when offered in payment, the whole debt was cancelled! Had this law regarded future contracts only, every man would have known on what terms to make his engagements; but to declare it legal to pay debts *already contracted*, with money of an inferior value, was altogether unjust!"

[2] "When the army was at Morristown, a man of respectable standing lived in the neighborhood, who was assiduous in his civilities to Washington, which were kindly received and reciprocated. Unluckily *this man paid his debts in the depreciated currency.* Some time afterwards he called at headquarters, and was introduced as usual to the General's apartment, where he was then conversing with some of his officers. He bestowed very little attention upon the visitor. The same thing occurred a second time, when Washington was more reserved than before. This was so different from his customary manner, that Lafayette, who was present on both occasions,

Two of my neighbors, Lieutenant Robert B. Wilkins and John Elliot, served in the war of the Revolution; the former was in the battle of Bunker Hill,[1] and in the course of the war served

could not help remarking it, and he said, after the man was gone, ' General, this man seems to be much devoted to you, and yet you have scarcely noticed him.' Washington replied, smiling, ' I know I have not been cordial; I tried hard to be civil, and attempted to speak to him two or three times, but that Continental money stopped my mouth.' "— Sparks' *Life of Washington*, p. 307.

[1] During the battle, suddenly feeling a pain in his right elbow, he said to a fellow-soldier near him, by whom he supposed he had been struck, " Hit the enemy with your gun and not *me*." He soon discovered that he had been hit by a bullet in his elbow. On being told by the surgeon who attended him that his arm must be amputated, his reply was, " It shall not be done." " Have you made your *peace* with God ? " inquired the chaplain. " With God," replied Wilkins, " I have never been at *war*." He retained possession of his arm; nevertheless his health was at length restored.

In 1780, when British soldiers committed great outrages in New Jersey, Lieutenant Wilkins was ordered to march at the head of a Company of American soldiers in quest of some of them. Calling one morning at the house of a widow, who was a Tory, living in New Jersey, and very well known to " give aid and comfort to the " British, he inquired of her whether there had been any enemies to our country in her house during the night ? " Wal," replied she, " there maught be and maught n't, I could n't say." After asking his question the third time, she invariably giving the same reply, he caused her house and barn to be set on fire, and this enemy's den was burnt to the ground. Lieutenant Wilkins and his Company then proceeded on their march, but were fired upon

as quartermaster in the detachment commanded by General Lafayette. He died August, 1832, aged 77 years. Elliot often had a great deal to say about the "Jarseys" in general, and of "Trentown" and "Princetown" in particular. He died Dec. 2, 1842, aged 87 years.

by a party of British soldiers from behind a fence. A fight between the two parties ensued, but the *Yankees* gained the victory. "The name of Yankee," said John Quincy Adams, "sometimes given to the people of New England in derision, was, in its origin, but the Indian pronunciation of the word *English;* and, whoever may at any time incline to couple it with a *sarcasm* or a *sneer*, IT IS THE GENUINE REPRESENTATIVE OF MANY OF THE NOBLEST QUALITIES THAT ELEVATE AND ADORN THE HUMAN CHARACTER."

CHAPTER III.

THE DEATH OF MY MOTHER. — MY ACADEMICAL CAREER.
— FATHER'S AND MY NAUTICAL ADVENTURE. — LIEU-
TENANT CHARITY LUND AND FAMILY. — FATHER'S SEC-
OND MARRIAGE. — HIS REMOVALS. — BROTHER ABEL'S
AND MY APPRENTICESHIP. — SIMON WILLARD. — I ES-
TABLISH THE CLOCK-MAKING BUSINESS IN CONCORD,
MAIN VILLAGE. — JOHN STEVENS.

MY mother died in Concord, N. H., Dec. 17, 1777, aged 41 years, when I was about six-teen years old, — an age when a child fully realizes such an irreparable loss. My father was absent from home when she died, but returned in time to attend the funeral. The words of Cowper, writ-ten on the receipt of his mother's picture, would express my thoughts if I were looking upon my mother's likeness: —

> "O that those lips had language! Life has passed
> With me but roughly since I heard thee last.
> Those lips are thine — thy own sweet smile I see,
> The same that oft in childhood solaced me!"

I saw my mother die! The poet's sentiment expresses my grief on this occasion: —

> "My mother! when I learned that thou wast dead,
> Say, wast thou conscious of the tears I shed?"

Seventy-seven years have passed since my mother died. Often have I thought of her during this time. " There were many ties that bound her to life, and she was one to feel those ties most tenderly, for her heart was open as the day, and responded most quickly to all the calls of friendship and affection. Her home was a happy and cheerful one, and she loved its inmates with a wife's and mother's fondness."

I had early enjoyed the advantages of attending common schools. Soon after my mother's death, my father placed me at Byfield Academy for one, and afterward at Andover Academy[1] for two, quar-

---

[1] While there he wrote a letter (directed " To Colonel Gordon Hutchins, at Concord, in New Hampshire, by the favor of Pomroy Lovejoy,") as follows :—

" *Andover, June 9th,* 1778.

" HONORED SIR : I have the opportunity to write to let you know that I am well and hope you are the same. I received your letter on the 6th inst., and enjoyed a great deal of pleasure in reading it.

" On the third day of this month, the house that Mr. Phillips dried his powder in was blown up ; he lost about two tons of powder, and three men were killed by the explosion, their legs and arms being blown off.

" I should be glad if you will bring me down some thread to half-foot my stockings with, a piece of cloth to mend my blue coat with, and some wafers. I cannot get any wafers here ; Mrs. Phillips has none ; she and all her family are well. I like living here very much. No more at present ; but I remain, your dutiful son,

Levi Hutchins

ters. Having paid the expenses attendant on my studies, he gave me a second-hand over coat, saying: —

"LEVI, THIS IS ALL I AM ABLE TO DO FOR YOU; AND NOW I HAVE GOT ONE PIECE OF ADVICE TO GIVE YOU: IN WHATEVER COMPANY YOU ARE, ALWAYS BE SURE THAT YOU PAY YOUR PART, AND ALWAYS KEEP GOOD COMPANY. IF YOU CANNOT AT FIRST GET INTO GOOD COMPANY, OBTAIN AS GOOD AS YOU DESERVE. WAIT UNTIL YOU DESERVE IT, AND YOU WILL BE SURE TO REACH IT."

Thus my father[1] committed me to the rough

[1] The following letter, received by him, relates to important *worldly* affairs: —

"*Exeter, June* 10*th*, 1778.

"COL. GORDON HUTCHINS: Sir, — After compliments, I would inform you that my Father, and Brother, and one Sister have returned home. They had the Small-Pox lightly. My other sister will be at home on Saturday next. There were 168 members of the present Academical Class, after having the disease slightly, inoculated. Another Class, how large I do not know, enters this week.

"Mr. Ward will call on you for 800 Clapboard nails, and 200 Brads, which please send to me, and I will see you satisfied. I suppose I shall be at Concord on Friday after next. The 'Portsmouth' is taken by the 'Experiment,' 50 guns. The 'Hornet,' built by Capt. Ladd, sent in a small but valuable Prize last night to Portsmouth. Night before last a French 20 Gunship got into Portsmouth. Mumford, the Post, saith that the British Forces are about leaving Philadelphia, but for what place they are bound he knows not. Please to give my Compliments to Mr. and Mrs. Hall. From your most Obsequious, most Obedient, and most Humble Servant, SAMUEL BROOKS, JR."

buffetings of the world; but I have sacredly cherished the remembrance of his advice, nay, the very words, as above, which he uttered in imparting it to me. A short time before I left Andover Academy, the Preceptor was asked by a man from Tewksbury, to name one of his best pupils, and my name was the one given him. The man then came to me and asked whether I would like to be a school-teacher? "Yes, sir, I should," was my reply. Consequently I taught school in Tewksbury, and afterward in Pembroke and Ashburnham; while so employed I enjoyed much happiness in the society of young people. Meantime, I regularly attended church, where singing constituted a part of the devotional exercises. I joined with the singers and "discoursed" music on my bass viol; this was worldly joy, and a Presbyterian minister likens sublunary joys to "the songs which peasants sing, full of melodies and sweet airs;" but those who possess another kind of joy, "go to heaven," he says, "not to the voice of a single flute, but to that of a whole band of instruments, discoursing wondrous music."

As every man's time is employed in various avocations, I would incidentally remark, that a letter, dated at Camp White Plains, Aug. 28, 1778, addressed to John White, Esq., at Blanchard's, Billerica, and signed J. Blanchard, contains the following words: "Your goodness prompts me to ask the favor of you to assist Col. Gordon

Hutchins, the bearer, in purchasing a small parcel of goods, which are to be brought on to this place, to such amount as you and he shall think proper. Col. Hutchins[1] will produce the money for the purpose, also for your trouble."

In 1779, my father and I shipped on board of a privateer, the " Hector," and, during our con-

---

[1] The following letter, which he received, is tinctured with an allusion to *matrimony*: —

" *Redding*, 21 *December*, 1778.

" COL. GORDON HUTCHINS: Dear Sir, — Your not coming to the Jerseys, as we talked of, made me Conjecture something unfavorable had Happened. I wrote you sundry short Letters, importing that I was well and stood ready to Execute any matters that you should request me to. But not hearing from you, I feared that your Letters and mine were Miscarried. I preserved a general silence in regard to my affairs, and Impatiently waited your Determination. But the increasing Confusion of the Times made me Think that you had Concluded not to Come here. I shall go to the Jerseys in a few days (if there is a possibility to Secure the Lands and Stores we talked of) and do myself the pleasure to call and see Mrs. Niell. I was told that *You were settling a family Compact with a Lady of Merrimac*. If this should be the case, I shall Reasonably suppose that it will be Advantageous to You and the Lady, and that it will, perhaps, Divert your attention from this way. I am now Paymaster, and shall continue to be for a while, but Hope there will be no Occasion for my services as Paymaster longer than next Spring or next Fall, at farthest. I most Earnestly Request you to write to me by every Opportunity, then perhaps some of your Letters will Reach me. I am in haste and write at Random, but am, with Affection, your Friend and Humble Servant, JAMES BLANCHARD."

tinuance in this vessel, I[1] officiated in the capacity of Doctor's Mate. We sailed from Salem, Mass., to the Penobscot River, near the mouth of which we dropped anchor. While lying off there we were informed of matters relative to privateering not advantageous to us. Soon afterward we saw English armed vessels pretty near us, and, not being in a condition to encounter a superior force, we sailed, pursued by our foe, up the river to the place where the city of Bangor is now located, though at that time there were but few buildings there; in 1772 the settlement contained but twelve families. At Bangor we disembarked from and blew up[2] our vessel! Then we escaped to the summit of an

[1] The following is an extract from a letter that he wrote to his father respecting this cruise: —

"*Pembroke*, —— 10*th*, 1779.

"HONORED SIR: I want to know whether I can go as Doctor's Mate, or Captain's Clerk? If you think I can go in either capacity, I should be very glad if you will send me a line about it. . . . Be so kind as to inform me how many shares a Clerk draws, if it will not be too much trouble to you. I send you, by Mr. Wait, your saddle-bags. . . . I remain, your most dutiful son,

Levi Hutchins

[2] This reminds one of an old ditty, in which are the words: —

"Fire on the main-top,
Fire on the bow,
Fire on the gun-deck,
Fire down below!"

almost perpendicular hill, taking hold of bushes, growing on its side, to aid our ascent. After the performance of this feat, which ended our public services in the war, my father and I set out on a long journey, and, after enduring much fatigue, arrived at our home in Concord, N. H. When in Bangor, a few years ago, I recognized the hill that father and I ascended in '79, and, in imagination, the scene of our escape from the "Hector" was again presented to my "mind's eye."

Between two and three years after my mother's death, my father formed a matrimonial connection with LUCY LUND, the eldest daughter of Lieutenant Charity Lund, of Merrimac, N. H., whose father, William, was a son of Thomas Lund, of Dunstable, N. H. This William, born in 1686, married Rachel ———, and was one of the first settlers in Merrimac. In 1723, o. s., he was taken by the Indians, and carried captive into Canada. During his captivity his wife, by her own exertions, converted such of her property as she best could into money, and gave five hundred livres, the price demanded, to Jacob Wendell,[1] of Boston, to be

---

[1] On receiving the money, he gave her a receipt as follows: —

                "*Boston, January 16th,* 1724–5.

"Received of Mrs. Rachel Lund, of Dunstable, Sixty Pound Bill Credditt, which she leaves with me in consideration of my giving my Letter of Credditt to Lieut. Joseph Blanchard, on Col. John Schuyler, att Albany; said Blanchard being bound to Canada for to get Mrs. Lund's Husband redeemed from the

appropriated by him for the redemption of her husband. He was redeemed and returned to his family after being absent a year. His wife used playfully to say to him, " You are truly *mine* for I *bought* you."[1] Their children were : William, born in 1717, Rachel, CHARITY, and Mary.

Lieutenant Charity Lund married Lucy ——; their children were : 1. Stephen, born May 14, 1754 ; 2. LUCY, born Sept. 24, 1756 ; 3. Eliza-

---

Indians. And if he does not make use of my Creddit, abovementioned, to the value of the sum she leaves with me, I promise to repay her the same.

" Per JACOB WENDELL."

On the evening of the 4th of September, 1724, o. s., the Indians fell on Dunstable and captured two men, Nathan Cross and Thomas Blanchard. A party, consisting of ten of the principal inhabitants of the town, went in search of them, under the direction of one French, their route being up the Merrimac River. At the brook near Lutwyche's (now Thornton's) Ferry, they were waylaid by the Indians who killed all but one of them. French was slain under an oak-tree standing in a field, which became the property of the late John Lund, of Merrimac. The tree, now standing, is directly east of the late Horatio Gates Hutchins' house, and about half way between it and the river.

[1] This brings to mind the following anecdote and stanza: Sylla obtained the prætorship partly by his assiduities and partly by his MONEY. While prætor, he said to Sextus Julius Cæsar, "I will use *my* authority against you." Cæsar replied, " You do well to call it *yours* for you *bought* it."

<blockquote>
" The golden hair that Galla wears
   Is hers ; who would have thought it ?
It must be hers, she so declares,
   And I know where she *bought* it."
</blockquote>

beth, born Feb. 14, 1758; 4. Rachel, born Jan. 14, 1760; 5. Charity, born Nov. 17, 1761; 6. Sarah, born July 6, 1763; 7. John,[1] born Sept. 6, 1765; 8. Hannah, born Feb. 6, 1767; 9. James, born May 29, 1768; 10. Cosmo, born Nov. 6, 1769; 11. Jeruthmeel, born May 2, 1771; 12. William, born Nov. 17, 1776; 13. Rebecca, born July 6, 1778.

Lieutenant Charity Lund possessed considerable property in Merrimac, where, at his house, I have often been kindly entertained by himself and family. His wife died Sept. 7, 1778. When my father, at the age of 46 years, asked him for the happiness of being married to his daughter Lucy, who was about 23 years of age, his enigmatical reply was, " Ah, I think that you are an old fool and that she is a young one."

The following marked lines represent the form of

[1] He married Mary Chambers, Feb. 17, 1811; he survived all of his brothers, and died Sept. 30, 1845, aged 80 years, and 24 days. She died Sept. 27, 1850, aged 75 years, 4 months, and 19 days. A friend of her husband wrote some stanzas on his death, two of which are as follows: —

" Our aged friend we've borne away,
   And laid him in his narrow bed;
Time passes sure without delay;
   His time, though long, at last has fled.

" The widow and the fatherless
   Did find in him a friend in need;
Long they his memory will bless,
   For he was thus a friend indeed."

4

a folded letter; the superscription and contents of the same were in my father's handwriting : —

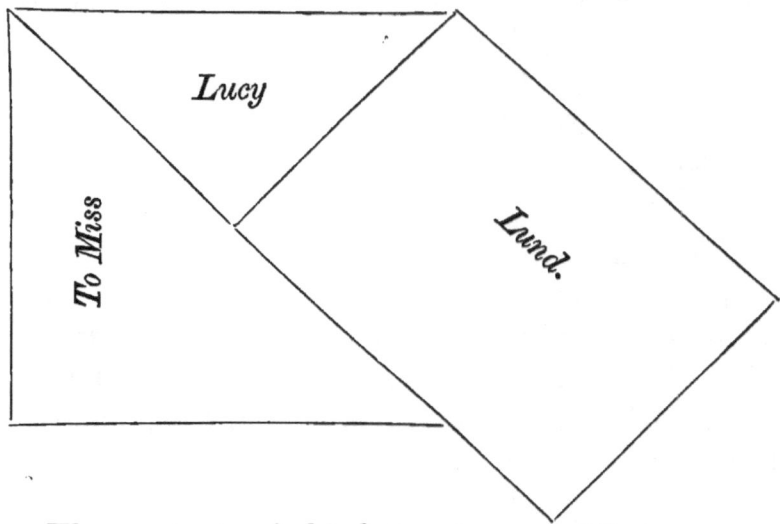

The contents of this letter were as follows : —

"*At Mr. Walker's, Wednesday, 4 P. M.*

"My dear : — *If agreeable to you I will wait on you, at eight o'clock this evening, at your Father's house. If not, please to write your name on this Paper and send it back by the Bearer. I am, Madam, your most obedient and very humble Servant,*

Gordon Hutchins

Lucy did not write her "name on this Paper, and," consequently, her "humble Servant, Gordon Hutchins," had the pleasure of her company.

In 1780, their marriage was consummated in Merrimac.

"COLONEL

GORDON HUTCHINS'

COMPLIMENTS:

INVITES

THE LADIES AND GENTLEMEN

TO SUP AT HIS COUNTRY SEAT,

On Friday, the 26th inst."

This card of invitation was written by my father soon after he married Lucy Lund, by whom he had five sons and four daughters, as follows, namely: Stephen, Nancy, Gordon, Lucy, Dolly, Horatio Gates, Betsy Tarbox, John Adams, and another Stephen.

A few months subsequent to this marriage, he moved to Pembroke, N. H., having previously engaged to superintend the management of a farm there and to take care of its owner, an aged man.[1]

---

[1] He took a lease of the farm for " two full years, from and after the first day of April, 1780." The Articles of Agreement were signed by him and the " aged man," Ambrose Goold, in presence of Benjamin Norris and Samuel Noyes, one item of the stipulation was, that " the said Hutchins shall pay one half of the Rates for the Real Estate," and in relation to which the following is a receipt: —

"January ye 14th, 1783, then received of Col. Gordon Hutchins one Pound 13s. 10d., L. M., it being his State, and County, and Town tax; it being his tax for the year 1782 for Pembroke.   BENJAMIN NORRIS, *Constable*."

While in Coventry, N. H., in 1782, Colonel Hutchins received a printed bill, passed in the New Hampshire Legislature, March 21, 1782, entitled " An Act for raising and

In this employment he so well acquitted himself, that the proprietor, some time before dying, left him the farm by will, which, however, the connections of the deceased old gentleman broke.

In 1783,[1] my father moved from Pembroke to

completing this State's Quota of the Continental Army," signed by John Langdon, *Speaker*, M. Weare, *President*, and Joseph Pearson, *Secretary*. On the back of it, in writing, was the following : —

               " *Concord, March* 27, 1782.

" COL. GORDON HUTCHINS : Sir, — The man for Coventry must be procured, if possible, and I will pay a suitable Proportion of the necessary Charge.

               " NATHANIEL PEABODY."

[1] The following letter, relating to a *nautical adventure*, before mentioned, is of some interest : —

               " *Pembroke*, 28 *April*, 1783.

" To CAPT. JOHN CARNES, of Salem : Sir, — After Compliments, I am to inform you, that I have heard of your repeated Misfortunes, for which I am heartily sorry, and I condole with you, as I always took you to be a gentleman of Honor and Probity. Doubtless, Sir, you remember that I went down on the Penobscot Expedition with an Intention to go out with you a Cruise on Board of the ' General Lincoln'; and that as you Disappointed me in this respect, you agreed to give me one full Share of whatever you made in said Cruise ; therefore whatever you can best spare of light Carriage, equal to said Share, please to deliver to the Bearer, Major Shaw, and it will be very gratefully received by him, who, in every shape and sense, is your Friend and Servant,

Gordon Hutchins

Coventry, where he built a grist-mill which, at length, he sold, and then moved to Haverhill, where, in 1786, he sold to Elisha Ensign "a tract of land lying in Sheffield, containing about four acres," for the sum of £17 10s.   Also, in 1787, for the sum of £12, he bought of Isaac Moore a "piece of wheat, in Peirmont, the same containing four acres."   In 1788, he "let unto Mary Bedal, of Haverhill, six sheep for the term of three years." After living in Haverhill several years, he moved to Rumney.   By the way, " Poor Richard" says : —

> " I never saw an oft-removed tree,
>   Nor yet an oft-removed family,
>   That throve so well as those that settled be."

" And, again, three removes are as bad as a fire." From Rumney my father moved to Concord, where he spent the remaining years of his life, his house being situated on the western side of the main village, a few rods from where the State House now stands.

My brother Abel and I, entertaining a desire to learn the same trade, commenced our apprenticeship, at clock-making, at nearly the same time. The name of the ingenious man of whom we learned this business was Simon Willard,[1] of Rox-

[1] A memoir of whom was prepared by Mr. Edward Holden, for the " New England Historical and Genealogical Society," and read at a meeting held in Boston, Sept. 2, 1857, of which the following is an abstract : —

Simon Willard, born in Grafton, Mass., April 3, 1753, was the seventh son in the family of twelve children of Benjamin

bury, Mass. One trait in his character was, I think, caution; for instance, during a thunder-

Willard. His mechanical genius was early developed. His father, disposed to encourage his design in cultivating it, placed him at the age of thirteen years under the instruction of a clock-maker of Grafton, by the name of Morris. In less than twelve months, Simon succeeded in constructing a complete and perfect clock, which was pronounced superior to those produced by his master.

In 1780, Mr. Willard, then twenty-seven years old, established himself in "Roxbury Street," opposite the present locality of the old clock-dial, erected by him in 1782. An act of the General Court of Massachusetts, passed July 2, 1782, granted to him the privilege of the exclusive manufacture and sale, for five years, of his clock-jack, an instrument which occupied an important place in the kitchen of many a gentleman of the old school.

A patent right for a timepiece of his invention was granted him, Feb. 8, 1802, by the National Government. Until the beginning of the present century, he devoted himself almost exclusively to the manufacture of the eight-day clock, and the estimated number of these clocks made by him is 200, and of timepieces 4000. Most of the tower-clocks, which ornament the churches and other public buildings in this and many other States of the Union, were either invented and constructed or improved by him. He made with his own hands, at the age of 82 years, the large clock for the Capitol at Washington. The machinery of the revolving lights on our extensive and dangerous coast were either designed and made or perfected by him. A large portion of the philosophical apparatus now in use at Harvard College, bears marks of his inventive powers or his perfecting skill. He constructed several musical clocks, which were arranged in such a manner as to play seven different tunes.

Mr. Willard was called to suffer domestic bereavement

storm he was particular in requiring his men and apprentices to suspend work in the shop, believing there was much danger to be apprehended, on such occasions, from the action of electricity, when using files and other metallic tools.   Thos. Jefferson sent to him from Virginia to make a clock for Charlotte College.   He made the clock, and, some time afterward, while at Mr. Jefferson's house, the latter asked him many questions concerning public affairs, with a view to test his knowledge of such matters; but his answers betraying ignorance, Mr. Jefferson plainly insinuated to him that he knew but little concerning them.   At length, by request of Mr. Jefferson, he took a French clock apart for the purpose of putting it in order, and laid the wheels, springs, and other portions on a table.   This done, he made preparations to go away.   " Do n't go, Mr. Willard," said the great statesman, "until you put the works of the clock together, for I cannot."   " Well," replied the clock-maker, " you seemed to think that I was quite ignorant of intricate public affairs, and so I concluded to let you try your skill in putting a clock together and make it keep good time.   This, however, you cannot do.

soon after passing the threshold of manhood, his wife dying at an early age, leaving one son.   On the 23d of January, 1788, he married Mary B. Leeds, of Dorchester, by whom he had eleven children.   He died in Boston, Sept. 20, 1848, in the 96th year of his age.   The prominent traits of his character were these: genius, mechanical skill, industry, honesty, and common sense.

So my knowledge of clock-making is about equal to your wisdom in State affairs."

After three years' apprenticeship under Mr. Willard, I[1] went to Abington, Ct., where I served eight months to acquire some knowledge of the art of repairing watches. Shortly afterward I returned to Concord, hired a shop on Main Street, purchased materials, and established the business of brass clock-making,[2] no person having before undertaken this enterprise in New Hampshire. As time passed, my trade in clocks increased, and I was encouraged by a successful beginning to do my best. At length, my business was suddenly interrupted by an Englishman named John Stevens, who endorsed a note for me. In 1777, he and several men were suspected of disaffection, published as enemies to the United States of America, confined in the jail at Exeter, and after a while released by taking the oath of allegiance. Having often heard from my father's lips patriotic expressions in favor of American Independence, and de-

---

[1] A lady, residing in Roxbury, informed me that she had often heard her mother speak in the highest terms of my father's personal appearance, agreeable manners, and good deportment during the time of his apprenticeship.

[2] From the "History of Concord" I learn, that Rev. Mr. Walker brought the first clock into that town from England. Dea. Joseph Hall, senior, owned the second clock in Concord, and there Ephraim Potter made *wooden* clocks, which were set up in some houses, about the year 1775, and later, and which kept good time.

nunciations of the enemies thereof, Stevens believed that he caused his apprehension and imprisonment, and so resolved to give *me* all the trouble he could, respecting the note, the payment of which I was not prepared to make at the time it became due. He paid the amount of the note, then attached all my property, and stopped my business entirely. However, I had friends, and, in a few weeks, they came with their money to my relief; the doors of my shop were unclosed and the clocks ticked again. I had taken Stevens [1] to be my friend, but his conduct proved him an enemy; yet "every time he fired a curse, I fired a blessing, and so we bombarded back and forth with this kind of artillery."

---

[1] Verily, in him *kindness faded away.* "I asked the red-hot iron, when it glimmered on the anvil, 'Wherefore glowest thou longer than the firebrand?' 'I was born in the dark mine, and the brand in the pleasant green-wood.' *Kindness fadeth away,* but VENGEANCE ENDURETH."

CHAPTER IV.

MARRIAGES, ETC., OF MY BROTHERS, ABEL AND EZRA, AND
OF MY SISTERS, BETHIAH, PAMELIA, AND MATILDA. —
BIRTHS, MARRIAGES, ETC., OF MY FATHER'S CHILDREN
BY HIS SECOND WIFE.

MY sister Bethiah was married in Concord,
N. H., March 13, 1783, to Dudley Ladd, a
hatter of Haverhill, Mass., where his father and
mother dwelt, and where he was born July 8, 1758.
His father, whose Christian name was Dudley, had
three daughters, named Alice, Harriet, and ———.[1]

[1] In the "History of Haverhill," Mass., is the following:
"A Mr. Ladd was engaged in the *hatting* business here,
[Haverhill], for many years previous to 1800; at which time
he was quite an old man. . . . Ladd, Appleton, and Marsh
made mostly 'fur beaver hats,' . . . The best fur hats cost
about seven dollars each, and were intended to last a lifetime.
A man usually purchased one with his wedding coat, and, in
most cases, he never had occasion to replace it. It was only
worn to meeting, and on great and special occasions. It was
put on and taken off by carefully taking hold of the buttons,
which held the turned-up rim, and from Sabbath day to Sabbath day again, with the exceptions mentioned, rested unmo-
lested upon its own particular peg in the 'front entry.'"

A Daniel Ladd was a Representative from Haverhill, in
the General Court, for the years 1693-4. A John Ladd was
one of the Selectmen of that town for the years 1747-8.

Bethiah's children were: —

1. Samuel Greenleaf,[1] born April 14, 1784, married Caroline Doliver Vinal, of Boston, Oct. 3, 1815. He settled in Hallowell, Me., and was Adjutant-General under Governor G. Kent.[2] 2.

[1] Colonel Gordon Hutchins was living in Haverhill, N. H., when he received the following letter: —

> *Concord, May* 5, 1784.

"HONORED FATHER: After our duty to you, we would inform you that we are comfortably well, thanks to Providence. We received your letter by Mr. Anderson, informing us that your son Stephen is dead. We hope the Lord will make you and your dear wife amends for your loss. We have no news to write you except that we have a fine little son, whom we have named *Samuel Greenleaf*. Our brother Abel Hutchins will probably be up to see you in June next, and perhaps we shall accompany him. From your Children,

Dudley Ladd
Bethiah Ladd

[2] Samuel Greenleaf Ladd moved from Hallowell, Me., to Kingston, Pa., where he died April, 1863, aged 79 years, and was buried at Laurel Hill Cemetery, near Philadelphia. His widow still lives in Kingston. Their children were: 1. Mary Caroline, who married Horatio Fairbanks, of Farmington, Me. In 1852, they emigrated to the Sandwich Islands, and sometime afterward to San Francisco, where he died Aug. 4, 1856, and where she deceased the following year, leaving two daughters, the oldest of whom resides in Boston, and was for several years a teacher in one of the public schools of that city. 2. Samuel. 3. Francis Dudley; he was a minis-

John, born Feb. 15, 1786, married Abigail Prowse,[1] of Portsmouth, N. H., April 4, 1807.   He died at

ter in the Episcopal Church, and for several years settled in Philadelphia, where he died July, 1862, from the effects of a fever brought on during his arduous and voluntary labors among the soldiers of the Federal Army of the Potomac.   4. Ellen, who married Rev. Henry Wells, of Kingston, Pa.   5. Theodore.   6. Charlotte, who married a Mr. Rose; they live in Minnesota.   7. Anna, who married a Mr. Fillebrown, of Lewiston, Me.   He entered the service of his country at the commencement of the present war, was Colonel of one of the Maine Regiments, and after its term of service expired he was appointed Provost-Marshal of Norfolk, Va.   8. Julia, who married a Mr. Titcomb, of Augusta, Me.; they live in Boston.   9. Augusta, who married Erastus F. Dana, formerly a merchant in Boston, but now residing in Chelsea, Mass. 10.   Horatio; he graduated at Bowdoin College, studied for the ministry at the Brunswick Theological Seminary, and was admitted to his profession.   He married, Aug. 5, 1863, Harriet Abbott, daughter of John S. C. Abbott, of New Haven, Conn., and is now a teacher in one of the public schools of New York City.   11. Henry; at the age of about thirteen years he fell upon the ice while skating, which caused his death.

[1] By his marriage to Abigail Prowse, he had three children : 1. William, who married a daughter of Ezekiel Goodale, of Hallowell, Me.; he emigrated with his family to the Sandwich Islands, in 1828, and was a merchant for many years in Honolulu, O. I., where he, his wife, and mother died in 1863.   2. Elizabeth, who married Aaron Palmer, of Concord, N. H.; they now live in Minnesota.   3. John; he married a Miss Nourse, a native of the State of Maine, and, in 1843, emigrated with his family to Honolulu, O. I., where for several years he had charge of the United States' Hospitals, and where he died in the Spring of 1861.

Valparaiso, July 26, 1824, aged 38 years. 3. Dudley,[1] born Aug. 19, 1789. 4. Nathanael Greene,[2] born Sept. 25, 1791. 5. William Manley,[3] born Feb. 9, 1794.

[1] He was twice married, first, May 21, 1823, to Charlotte Eastman, daughter of Ebenezer Eastman, of Salisbury, N. H.; she died Jan. 30, 1826, aged 27 years, leaving one child, Charlotte Eastman Ladd, who married Edward H. Barrett, of Warner, N. H.; they live in New Boston, Minnesota. Dudley Ladd had for his second wife, Amanda Palmer, of Orford, N. H.; they were married Dec. 24, 1837; their children are : 1. Ellen Frances, who married Daniel F. Murphey, of Marlborough, Mass., June 15, 1863. 2. Harriet Louisa; she graduated at the Salem, Mass., Normal School, and is now a teacher. 3. Julia Amanda; she married George Baker, of Franklin, N. H., August, 1862; they live in South Boston, Mass. 4. Maria Fletcher. 5. Charles Dudley.

[2] He married, May 14, 1817, Anne Morrow, of New York City, where he settled and there died December, 1863, aged 72 years. Their children were : 1. Ann Bethiah, who married Edward Luff; she died in 1864. 2. Lucinda Parsons; she married David Patterson, of Staten Island, N. Y. 3. Eleanor Lewis; she married Austin A. Hall, a merchant in the city of New York, where they reside. 4. William Dudley; he married Mary Ann Emerson, of Franklin, N. H.; they now live in Concord, N. H., and his business is that of a hardware merchant. 5. Mary Jane, who married M. D. L. Sharkey, of New York City, died at the age of 20 years. 6. George and Sarah (twins); Sarah married William Corwin, of New York. 7. Nathanael. 8. Julia.

[3] He was formerly a bookbinder and bookseller in Concord, N. H.; he married, Nov. 20, 1822, Betsy Collins, of Lynn, Mass., where they reside. Their children are : 1. William Henry, who was twice married, first to Jane Pearsons, of Cambridge, Mass., where he was a teacher in the Shepard

Bethiah and her husband lived many years in Concord, where they owned real estate, but finally moved to Franklin, N. H., where their son Dudley and his family live. Bethiah died in that town Jan. 29, 1835, aged 69 years, and 4 months. Her husband died in the same town Dec. 23, 1841, aged 83 years, 5 months, and 15 days.

My brother Abel married Elizabeth Partridge, of Roxbury, Mass., Jan. 22, 1786. They lived together, in Concord, N. H., sixty-seven years, and had five sons and eight daughters, as follows: — Charles, Sally Gridley, Dolly, Catharine, Eliza, George, Jane Johnson, Lewis, Ephraim, Hamilton, Mary Ann, Hannah Taylor, and Martha Currier; of whom the following is an account: —

1. Charles, born Nov. 6, 1787, married, Jan. 5, 1808, Hannah Taylor, daughter of Nathan Taylor, Esq., of Sanbornton, N. H. She died Dec. 28, 1810, aged 23 years, and 15 days. She had one child, Nathan Taylor Hutchins, born Oct. 31, 1808. This child died Feb. 6, 1809. Charles afterward married Mary Thorndike, daughter of Dr. John Thorndike, of Concord; he lives in Concord, where for several years he has been engaged in mercantile business.

School about five years; she died about a year after their marriage, leaving one child, Mary Holman Ladd. In 1856, he married Martha Gregory, also of Cambridge; they live in Lynn, Mass., where he is a teacher in Chauncy Hall School.
2. Ann Elizabeth.

2. Sally Gridley, born July 3, 1788, married Warren Lovejoy,[1] a merchant of Boston.

3. Dolly, born July 18, 1790, married Isaac Danforth,[2] a merchant of Boston, but afterward of Concord, N. H.

4. Catharine, born July 21, 1792, married William Kent,[3] a merchant of Concord, son of Colonel William A., and brother of ex-governor Kent, of Maine; she died March 12, 1839.

5. Eliza, born Nov. 16, 1794, married Samuel N. Baker,[4] of Ipswich, Mass.

[1] Their children were: 1. Sarah; 2. Catharine; 3. Mary Ann, who married James Tallant; their children were: Charles, George, Valina, Ella, and Hamilton; 4. Martha, who married Philip Eastman; their children were: Susan, Kate, Charles Henry, Willie, and Nellie; 5. Charles, who married Eliza Jones, of Boston; their children were: Frederic, Charles, and Mary Elizabeth.

[2] Their children were: 1. James, who married Mary Jane Wellington, of Lexington, Mass.; 2. George, who married Fannie Wright, of Pittsfield, Mass.; their children were: Fannie, Herbert, Harry, Charlie, Mary, and Jessie; 3. Isaac Warren, who married Eliza Hastings, daughter of Oliver Hastings, of Cambridge, Mass.; 4. Elizabeth; 5. Mary Jane; 6. Charles.

[3] Their children were: 1. Austin, who married Isabella N. Bartley, of New Orleans; 2. Augusta, who married O. Wellington; 3. Lucy Jane, who married A. Wellington; 4. Henry W., who married Hattie Farnum, of Bangor, Me.; 5. Mary, who married N. Halleck, of New York; 6. John; 7. Ellen, who married Henry Muzzey; 8. Charles, who married Lizzie Bridgeman, of Boston; 9. Frank; 10. Prentiss.

[4] Their children were: 1. Eliza, who married H. Danniels;

6. George, born Oct. 21, 1797, married to Sarah R. Tucker,[1] is a merchant of Concord, N. H.

7. Jane Johnson, born July 15, 1799, married Colonel Robert Ambrose,[2] a merchant of Concord, N. H., and son of Stephen Ambrose, Esq.

8. Lewis, born Sept. 30, 1801, died at Wetumpka, Ala., in 1839, aged about 38 years.

9. Ephraim, born Oct. 4, 1803, married to Elizabeth Blodgett,[3] of Randolph, Vt., lives in Concord, where he kept the Phœnix Hotel several years.

10. Hamilton,[4] born July 10, 1805. He gradu-

---

2. Hannah; 3. Joanna; 4. Jane; 5. John; 6. Samuel; 7 Sarah; 8. Kate.

[1] Their children were: 1. Sarah Elizabeth; 2. George Ridgeway; 3. Sarah Jane; 4. Mary Thorndike, who married Franklin Low; 5. Abel Hutchins, who married Mary C. Reed; 6. George Hamilton, who married Susan A. Williams; 7. Benjamin Tucker, who married Alice Green; 8. Charles Lewis; 9. Edward Ridgeway; 10. Sarah Francis.

[2] Their children were: 1. George, who married Elizabeth Little, of Portland, Me.; 2. Charles, who married Jannette Emerson, of Fryburgh, Me.; 3. Nancy; 4. Robert, who married Julia Davis, of Portland, Me.

In 1829 and 1830, Colonel Ambrose represented the town of Concord in the State Legislature. In September, 1831, while riding over the Mill Dam, from Boston to Roxbury, he was thrown from his vehicle, causing a fracture of his skull which produced immediate death.

[3] Their children were: 1. Robert; 2. Elizabeth, who married Augustus Shuts, of Coquimbo, Chili; 3. Gordon; 4. Hamilton; 5. Carroll.

[4] He married Mary Chandler, of Lexington, Mass. She died a short time after marriage. He died April 6, 1851.

ated from Dartmouth College, N. H., and from the military institution at Norwich, Vt., and was admitted to the bar at Concord, N. H., in 1830.

11. Mary Ann, born June 1, 1807. She lives in Concord, N. H.

12. Hannah Taylor, born Dec. 22, 1810, married Augustine C. Pierce,[1] of Concord, N. H. She died in 1853.

13. Martha Currier,[2] born March 1, 1813.

My sister Pamelia[3] married Daniel Craig, son of Alexander Craig, of Exeter, N. H., Dec. 13, 1793. Soon after marriage they moved to Rumney, N. H. He was born Feb. 5, 1771, and died March 13, 1814, aged 43 years, 1 month, and 8 days. They had five sons and three daughters,[4] as follows : —

1. Sarah, born Oct. 9, 1797 ; 2. Lavinia, born July 27, 1800 ; 3. Nancy H., born May 6, 1802 ; 4. John, born Nov. 10, 1803 ; 5. Gilbert, born June 20, 1805 ; 6. Samuel G., born June 20, 1807 ; 7. Oliver W., born April 3, 1809 ; 8. Daniel H., born Nov. 3, 1811.

[1] Their children were : 1. Julia Hutchins ; 2. Lewis ; 3. Martha.

[2] She married A. C. Pierce, by whom she had a daughter named Mary Hamilton.

[3] She was the last survivor of the family, and died in Rumney, N. H., Jan. 15, 1859, aged 86 years, 5 months, and 14 days.

[4] One of these daughters married Solomon Jones, of Rumney, N. H., and one of the sons, by this marriage, namely, Greenleaf C. Jones, married Annie L. March, of Hebron, N. H., Dec. 1, 1863.

My brother Ezra married [1] Sarah, widow of Mr. —— Currier, and daughter of Benjamin Lamson, of Exeter, N. H., who died, in 1817, aged 79 years, in Concord, N. H., where his remains now repose in the old burial-ground. By her marriage with Mr. Currier, Sarah had a daughter, Martha, who married Nathan Stickney, of Concord, N. H. Martha, a daughter by the latter union, married Edward Pendexter, of Madbury, N. H.

Ezra lived a while in Concord, N. H., after his marriage, and then moved to Exeter, N. H. His children were: 1. Clarissa Lamson, born Dec. 10, 1797, in Concord, N. H.; 2. Mary Parker, born July 10, 1799, in Exeter, N. H.; 3. Dolly,[2] born June 10, 1802, in Exeter, N. H.

[1] At my request, the Town Clerk of Exeter examined its Records from 1648 to 1830, inclusive, under the heads of Publishments, Births, Marriages, and Deaths, and found that the name of Hutchins appears but once on these records, as follows: —

"Married, in Exeter, Feb. 26, 1797, by William F. Rowland, Mr. Ezra Hutchins and Mrs. Sarah Currier, of this town."

[2] She married Richard Potter, Esq., June 18, 1840, and died at Bangor, in 1862, aged about 40 years. The following are extracts from one of her letters to me, dated at that city, April 5, 1859: —

. . . "I have not forgotten you nor 'the web of ropes' and the many good times that we had together, when children, at my father's house and also at yours. . . . Oh! what changes have transpired, in both families, since the days of our youth. We had one visit from your brother John, and we should be pleased to see you here. Write again and again to me. The

In April, 1806, Ezra moved back to Concord and purchased and settled on a farm, on " Diamond's Hill." In 1810, my youngest son, Samuel, and I rode in a sleigh, one winter afternoon, to his house there. I intended to return home in the evening, but the social circle of my brother's household, cheered by the mingled light of the bright wood-fire and of his domestic tallow-candles, caused so much happiness, that I was induced to postpone our return till morning.[1] In the midst of our enjoyment, at about seven o'clock, my little boy, after looking through a window to see the snow below and the moon and stars above, said to me, " Come, come, I wish to go home, not because I am homesick for I am really happy ; but I want to ride in the sleigh by moonlight." At the close of this earnest speech, we all laughed most heartily. Ezra, thinking that the author of this hilarity deserved a reward, offered him half a dozen coppers, which were respectfully refused. Our merriment would have reminded a person outside, of the good scrip-

chain of love and friendship, which used to bind our families together, should be kept bright and unbroken." . . .

[1] The following lines are applicable to this description : —

> " Now stir the fire, and close the shutters fast,
> Let fall the curtains, wheel the sofa round,
>
> .   .   .   .   .
>
> So let us welcome joyful evening in.
>
> .   .   .   .   .
>
> O Winter, ruler of the inverted year,
> I crown thee king of intimate delights,
> Fireside enjoyments, homeborn happiness."

tural passage : " *When the Lord turned again the captivity of Zion, then was our mouth filled with laughter.*"

My sister Matilda was but 2 months and 6 days old when her mother died. A Mrs. Dix, of Boscawen, N. H., adopted her, and she lived in her family until Feb. 9, 1800, when she married Noah Greely Wiggin, a hatter of that town. Shortly afterward, they moved to Amherst, N. H., and, subsequently, to Bath, Me., where he died Oct. 13, 1813 ; soon after this event she moved to Concord, N. H., where she died Feb. 4, 1819, aged 41 years, 4 months, and 23 days. They had six children as follows : —

1. The first child, born Oct. 15, 1800, died in infancy ; 2. Timothy Dix,[1] born Sept. 25, 1801, died Nov. 21, 1846 ; 3. Caroline, born March 30, 1804, died Dec. 6, 1808 ; 4. Margaret Sargent,[2] born Oct. 29, 1806 ; 5. Matilda Greely, born Feb. 2, 1809, died Oct. 14, 1850 ; 6. Sarah Greely Hutchins, born July 9, 1811, died July, 1840.

[1] He married Elizabeth Partridge, of Roxbury, Mass., whose father was a brother of Elizabeth Partridge, wife of my uncle Abel Hutchins.

[2] She married, April 13, 1837, Phineas B. Smith, of Roxbury, Mass., where they now live. Their children are: 1. Phineas Bean, Jr.; he was born Feb. 6, 1838, married, Nov. 5, 1863, and now lives in Roxbury, Mass.; 2. Nathan Gilman, born March 30, 1840; 3. Marcus Morton, born Jan. 9, 1843; 4. Sarah Margaret, born Jan. 25, 1847; 5. Henry Augustus, born June 29, 1850.

In 1845, my brother Abel, brother Ezra, sister Pamelia, and myself had a meeting in Concord, N. H., the first occasion upon which we had all been together since the year 1776, a period of sixty-nine years. Our united ages, at the time of this meeting, amounted to three hundred and thirteen years, equal to seventy years and three months for each one of us.

The following is an account of my father's children by his second wife, Lucy : —

1. Stephen, born Nov. 27, 1780, was taken sick March 24, 1784, and died April 5, following, aged 3 years, 4 months, and 8 days. A sermon was preached on the occasion of his funeral, by Rev. Mr. Richards, pastor of the Church in Peirmont.

2. Nancy,[1] born July 10, 1782, married Ben-

[1] The following are extracts from some of her letters to her parents : —

"*Rumney, Sept.* 16, 1801.

. . . "I have had a very agreeable visit. The people were glad to see me, and desired me to keep a school, in Mr. Haynes' district, for the sum of one dollar per week." . . .

"*Rumney, May* 26, 1802.

. . . "I have no news to write except we have not moved yet. We live in the house with my husband's brother." . . .

"*Rumney, June* 27, 1805.

. . . "I am going to send you, dear mamma, a piece of checked cambric for a gown for myself. I want Mrs. Tuttle to cut it out and fix it for me in the newest fashion. She can fit it to you for yours fitted me last winter." . . .

"*Buffalo, Nov.* 14, 1813.

. . . "The wished-for time draws nigh when I shall revisit the place of my nativity. . . . Our fears about being disturbed

jamin Haynes. She died in Buffalo, N. Y., July
2, about 10 o'clock, p. m., 1814, aged 32 years,
11 months, and 22 days. "She was sensible that
she was dying," wrote her husband to her parents,
"and requested me to send you certain articles of
hers. . . . Just at the moment she expired, our
troops were marching by my house toward Canada.
. . . I pray you may be supported by Divine grace
in sustaining the loss of your dearly beloved daughter." . . .

The following is a copy of a notice, read in
church, in relation to her death : —

"Gordon Hutchins and his wife desire the
prayers of the good people of Concord, that God
will sanctify unto them His holy hand of Providence in taking one of their daughters away by
death."

3. Gordon, Jr., was born April 5, 1785, in Concord, N. H., where he learned the saddler's trade ;
sometime afterward he carried on the business in
Amesbury, Mass., where he married Abigail Sargent, daughter of Zebulon Sargent. By this marriage he had two children, Erastus,[1] and Abby

by war are less than they were. General Harrison, who went
to the West, returned, not long since, with seven vessels loaded
with British prisoners. It was a beautiful scene to behold the
vessels come in ; it was a day of rejoicing ; at night the village
was handsomely illuminated. I have lately seen several Eng-
lishmen who were taken by the Indians during the old war ;
they have squaws for wives and they dress like Indians." . . .

[1] He lives in Derry, N. H.

Jane.[1] Gordon, Jr.,[2] died in Buffalo, N. Y., Aug. 17, 1817, aged 32 years, 4 months, and 2 days. Several years after his decease, his widow married Stephen Clement,[3] of Amesbury, Mass.

4. Lucy, born Nov. 26, 1787, married, Jan. 26, 1806, David Webster,[4] of Plymouth, N. H. Soon

---

[1] She married Benjamin F. French, of Deerfield, N. H., son of Peter P., and grandson of Benjamin French, of Epping, N. H., who served as a Lieutenant in the Revolutionary War. Abby Jane and her husband live in Haverhill, Mass.; they have one son, named Frank.

[2] His parents received a letter, dated at Oswego Village, N. Y., March 26, 1815, in which were these words: "Your son, Gordon, a saddler by trade, is sick with consumption, and in need of pecuniary assistance." Soon after receiving this intelligence, they wrote their son a letter, from which the following are extracts: —

. . . "The feelings of our hearts, dearly beloved son, concerning your distressed situation, we cannot express. . . . We must leave you in the hands of a merciful God, in whom we hope you will put your trust. With gratitude we return our sincere thanks to those friends who have helped you. . . .

Gordon & Lucy Hutchins

[3] He died in 1861. Since this year she has lived in Haverhill with her daughter, and son-in-law, Abby Jane and B. F. French.

[4] Their children (besides the first two, who died in their infancy) were: 3. Saloma, born April 23, 1809, married David W. Doyc, March 27, 1832; 4. Dardane, born June 25, 1812, died Aug. 11, 1814; 5. Emeline M. and Adeline M. (twins), born May 1, 1815. Adeline M. died Oct. 27, 1831. Emeline M. married Ichabod P. Hardy, Feb. 2, 1836;

after marriage they moved to Danville, Vt., and there dwelt until Feb. 10, 1815, when they moved to Rumney, N. H., where he died May 15, 1849. The remembrance of my happy visits at their house in Rumney, where his widow[1] still lives, I fondly cherish. He was a farmer.

5. Dolly, born May 15, 1790, died in Nashua, N. H., Sept. 25, 1825, aged 35 years, 4 months, and 10 days, leaving a husband and children.

6. Horatio Gates, born June 10, 1792, married, May 20, 1824, Abigail Barrett,[2] who was born

---

7. David P., born Oct. 3, 1817, married Mary Preston, Jan. 12, 1840; 8. Elizabeth H. C. M., born April 8, 1820, married David P. Hadley, May 12, 1841; 9. Nancy H., born April 22, 1824, married J. W. Peppard, Oct. 22, 1862.

[1] The following are extracts from two of her letters to her parents: —

"Danville, Vt., Feb. 16, 1807.

. . . "How shall I express my sorrow to you concerning the death of my little son ? . . . This is the first trouble that I ever had ; he was born on the 21st day of Oct. last and died on the 29th." . . .

"Danville, Vt., Feb. 17, 1809.

. . . "I wish, dear parents, you could come and see us. It seems as if my brother Horatio and sister Betsy might come. . . . Our children are well, grow fast, and are now playing together on the floor. How much I do love them." . . .

[2] Their children were : 1. Mary Lund, born Nov. 15, 1825, married Charles P. Taft, Sept. 1, 1852 ; 2. John Lund, born May 24, 1828 ; for several years he has been living in California, —

"Where rivers roll o'er golden sand,
And forests sway'd by breezes bland,
With garlands gay are hung."

June 28, 1804. I have often visited them at their house in Merrimac, N. H., where he owned and cultivated a good farm. During my last visit there, he said, " Oh! Levi, how much I desire to see, ONCE more, the place in Concord where my parents lived." He died Jan. 31, 1850, aged 57 years, 7 months, and 21 days. It was justly said of him, in a Nashua, N. H., newspaper,[1] that " He was a

3. Horatio Gates, born June 21, 1835, died May 14, 1855, aged 19 years, 10 months, and 23 days. His body was buried near his father's remains, in the burial-ground of his native town, and " rests by the Merrimac's bright wave." He possessed many excellent qualities of mind and heart, and manifested a maturity of thought beyond his years; 4. Abigail Barrett, born Oct. 4, 1838, died Feb. 2, 1840; 5. Another son, born May 18, 1843, died in infancy.

[1] In this paper were the following lines in memory of him : —

" He was a man of virtue's cast,
    And bright is left the spell,
That long will linger in the past
    And with affection dwell.

" 'T was his to tread an even way,
    Through every changing scene ;
His faith was like a beacon ray
    Upon a silver stream.

" 'T was his to love his fellow-men,
    As well as kindred dear ;
His cheerful task has often been
    To wipe the falling tear.

" The living may indeed lament
    The loss of such a friend,
And sigh that he could not be lent
    A longer life to spend."

worthy citizen, a kind and obliging neighbor, and respected for his integrity and industry wherever known. His loss is deeply lamented by a large circle of neighbors and friends."

7. Betsy Tarbox,[1] born March 12, 1794, married David V. Chambers, a farmer of Vermont, where they live.

8. John Adams,[2] who was born April 17, 1798, died in Merrimac, N. H.

[1] The following are extracts from two of her letters: —

"*Merrimac, Sept.* 6, 1814.

"DEAR PARENTS: My heart dilates with joy at the pleasing prospect of seeing you again this fall. Oh! you cannot imagine how much I have thought of you since I received the melancholy intelligence of the death of my sister Nancy. . . . How kindly you have ever regarded the welfare of your children." . . .

"*Randolph, Vt., May* 1, 1819.

"DEAR SISTER LUCY: These lines are to inform you that my family is in a comfortable state of health. You undoubtedly heard that my son Isaac died on the 19th day of December last, leaving a widow and two sons. My sons, Elhanan, and Lund Tarbox, are at home. Elhanan thinks of going on a sea-voyage soon. . . . I hope that you and all of my brothers and sisters are well; may you all enjoy, as the gift of our Heavenly Father, that peace which the world can neither give nor take away." . . .

[2] He married Catharine Nowell, by whom he had three children: 1. Gordon, who died in childhood; 2. Elhanan Winchester, who married Priscilla Cheever, and lives with his family in East Cambridge, Mass.; 3. Lucy Frances, who married A. P. Gilson, and lives with her family in Manchester, N. H.

9. Stephen, born Nov. 13, 1801, married Mary S. Avery,[1] March 12, 1837. He formerly pursued the business of farming in Merrimac,[2] and now continues it in Rumney, N. H.

[1] They had nine children, the first two dying in their infancy; the seven others were as follows : —

3. Alonzo G., born June 2, 1841; 4. Mary E., born June 25, 1843; 5. Harriet, E., born Sept. 4, 1846; 6. Nancy H., born Dec. 5, 1848; 7. Elhanan W., born March 1, 1853; 8. Clara J., who was born July 28, 1855, died July 29, 1857; 9. Francis E., born March 3, 1858.

[2] Rev. Jacob Burnap, D. D., who graduated at Harvard University, in 1770, was pastor of the First Congregational Church in Merrimac for almost fifty years, and used to remark, that Merrimac furnished not less than forty strong, athletic men who were employed in active service in some portion of the war of the Revolution. Besides other men of note, who formerly lived in Merrimac, were John McGaw, Esq., " a useful member of society, and a staid and exemplary Christian," and Matthew Thornton, a signer of the Declaration of Independence, and afterward Chief Justice of the Court of Common Pleas, and Judge of the Superior Court of New Hampshire.

CHAPTER V.

DESCRIPTION OF THE MAIN VILLAGE OF CONCORD, N. H. — THE RELIGIOUS DENOMINATION OF FRIENDS. — THE HANNAFORD FAMILY, THEIR BIRTHS, MARRIAGES, ETC.

BEFORE I state the particulars of my marriage, which came next in course to my brother Abel's, other subjects must be briefly noticed, as follows: When, in 1772, I first saw the Main Village of Concord, the buildings composing it were scattered over a large area of ground, but the most of them were situated, for the distance of a mile and a half, on both sides of the road running north and south near to and parallel with the Merrimac River; from this circumstance, the appellation of "The Street" was given to the whole village. It is customary now, as formerly, to say, referring to this part of Concord, "I live in ' The Street,'" or, "I am going to ' The Street.'" The Merrimac River flows through the whole length of Concord from north to south, and, in its course to the ocean, furnishes an immense water power. Indeed, no river on this continent propels so much

machinery as this.[1] Various business transactions
have led me to travel throughout the State of New
Hampshire, and I have derived great pleasure from
viewing its mountains, hills, and valleys.[2] Eighty-
two years ago, in 1772, I did not dream of the
CHANGES[3] that have since taken place in Concord.

1 "THE MERRIMAC."

" Oh, child of that white-crested mountain, whose springs
    Gush forth in the shade of the cliff-eagle's wings,
    Down whose slopes to the lowlands thy wild waters shine,
    Leaping gray walls of rock, flashing thro' the dwarf pine.

              .   .   .   .   .

" Oh, Stream of the Mountains! if answer of thine
    Could rise from thy waters to question of mine,
    Methinks through the din of thy thronged banks a moan
    Of sorrow would swell for the days which have gone.

" Not for thee the dull jar of the loom and the wheel,
    The gliding of shuttles, the ringing of steel;
    But that old voice of waters, of bird and of breeze,
    The dip of the wild-fowl, the rustling of trees! "
                                                    Whittier.

2 The following are the names of some of the mountains,
hills, lakes, ponds, villages, &c., of New Hampshire : Owl-head,
Baldface, Double-head, and Squam mountains; Squanagon-
nic, Cobble, Bald, and Brimstone hills; Mount Misery; the
Devil's Den; the Devil's Slide ledge; Bungtown, and Swift-
water villages; Squam, and Umbagog lakes; Massabesic, and
Bear ponds; Blow-me-down, and Roaring brooks. The Indians gave to one of the small rivers of the State this name :
    QUOHQUINAPASSAKESSANANNAGNOG.

3 It has been said, that " Time hath power to change the
pulses of the heart." It also has power to change the appearance of towns. John Adams, when a young man, wrote
to a friend as follows: "All that part of creation, which lies

In 1775 the whole township contained only 1050
inhabitants; the population has now increased to
more than ten times this number. In 1805 it
became the seat of Government of New Hampshire,[1] and in 1823 the County seat of Merrimac.
But the Main Village or "Street" is the most important part of Concord. Among its many shops
for mechanical business is a large establishment for
the manufacture of carriages. Its humble stores
and taverns, of days long past, though good, were
unlike its magnificent stores and hotels of to-day.
The City of Concord now contains four Banks,
with an aggregate capital of $430,000, two Savings
Institutions, three Fire Insurance Companies, an
Asylum for the Insane, nine or ten Church edifices,
several printing-offices, bookstores, &c.

The State Prison, built in 1811–12, and afterward enlarged and improved, consists of four build-

within our observation, is liable to change. If we look into
history, we shall find some nations rising from contemptible
beginnings, and spreading their influence till the whole globe
is subjected to their sway. When they have reached the
summit of grandeur, some minute and unsuspected cause
commonly effects their ruin, and the empire of the world is
transferred to some other place. Immortal Rome was at first
but an insignificant village, inhabited only by a few abandoned ruffians; but by degrees it rose to a stupendous height,
and excelled, in arts and arms, all the nations that preceded
it."

[1] In 1775, the population of the State, according to con-
jectural estimates, was 102,000. Its population by the last
census was 317,976.

ings, which, with the yard, covers an area of two acres, surrounded by a granite wall.

The State House, commenced in 1816, and completed in 1819, occupies a large plot of ground, ornamented with trees, extending from Main to State Street, and enclosed by an iron railing. The exterior walls are of hammered granite.

The ancient edifice (about which I stated a few particulars in recounting some of my father's military services, in 1777,) where Rev. Israel Evans, Rev. Timothy Walker, Rev. Asa McFarland, and Rev. Nathaniel Bouton, D. D., formerly preached many sermons, well known by the name of the " Old North Church," is situated at the north end of " The Street," and is now occupied as a Methodist General Biblical Institute.

The Old Court House was erected in the Main Village when I was but thirty years old, and the work of enlarging it commenced when my years numbered just sixty.

In thinking of past things, I am reminded that Peter Green and others were granted by the Legislature of New Hampshire the exclusive right of building a bridge over the Merrimac River, a short distance above the south line of Concord. The stock, divided into one hundred shares, was subscribed for by seventy-six persons, including my brother Abel and myself. The bridge cost something over $13,000. On its completion, Oct. 29, 1795, a procession of men, accompanied by a band of music, marched across it and partook of a dinner at William Stickney's tavern.[1]

The religious denomination of Friends was, for many years, from the time of its foundation in England, by GEORGE FOX, about the middle of the 17th century, derisively treated and shamefully persecuted by other Christian denominations. In 1662, there was some trouble in Dover, N. H., caused by the enmity of Calvinists toward those who promulgated the doctrines of Friends. Some women of that town, having publicly embraced the new religion, were barbarously sentenced to receive ten lashes on the naked back! But *arguments* of this kind had the effect to increase the number of Friends in Dover. A Friend of Epping, N. H., by the name of Charles Norris, was imprisoned because he most resolutely refused to pay taxes toward supporting a Calvinistic church of that town. He wisely thought that his religious opponents should, themselves, defray their expenses in disseminating their doctrines. Among other practices, upheld by some Christians and discountenanced by Friends, is that of dancing. In 1724, a Friend named Downs, was unfortunately taken prisoner by the Indians; his refusal to *dance*, as

[1] About fifty-four years ago, when Mr. George Peabody, the wealthy London banker, was but twelve years old, he passed through Concord and stopped at this tavern, where he paid for his lodging and breakfast by sawing wood. Several years ago, during his visit to the United States, he gave more than half a million of dollars to public objects.

he was commanded to do, subjected him to gross insults. In New Hampshire there are now fifteen societies of Friends.

Benjamin Hannaford[1] was born in Haverhill, Mass., May 14, 1735. When about twenty-two years old, having learned the carpentering business, he enlisted, fought against the French and Indians, and was captured by them; but making his escape he returned to Haverhill. He was twice married; first, to Ruth Page,[2] of Haverhill; they had six children as follows:—

[1] From the " History of Haverhill," and from the records of that town, it appears that his father's name was *Zachariah* Hannaford, who married, in Haverhill, Oct. 12, 1732, Mary Greely or Grealee; their children were: 1. Mary, born at Stratum, Oct. 16, 1733; 2. BENJAMIN, born May 14, 1735; 3. Abigail, born July 10, 1737; 4. Miriam, born Feb. 25, 1739, o. s.; 5. Zachariah, born May 4, 1742; 6. Anna, born Sept. 26, 1744; 7. Joseph, born March 4, 1746, died Dec. 19, 1749; 8. Elizabeth, born Aug. 8, 1750; 9. Joseph, born April 14, 1753; 10. John, born Aug. 15, 1757, died Nov. 2, 1762.

[2] John Hutchins married, Nov. 11, 1695, Sarah Page; both of Haverhill; their children were: John, Sarah, Richard, James, Jeremiah, David, Mary, Jonathan, Nathaniel, and Elizabeth. In the list of Representatives from Haverhill to the State Legislature, for the year 1697, is the name of John Page. Richard Hutchins married, Oct. 2, 1727, Martha Greely; both of Haverhill; their children were: Ezekiel and Abigail. James Hutchins married, Nov. 12, 1729, Ruth Greely; their children were: Sarah, Willford, Jeremiah, Ruth, and William. Hezekiah Hutchins, of Newbury, married, Jan. 29, 1761, Anne Swett, of Haverhill.

1. John, born May 5, 1763, died Oct. 3, 1777;
2. James, born Jan. 4, 1765, died —; 3. PHEBE,
born April 15, 1766; 4. Greely, born Nov. 19,
1767; 5. Ruth, born June 21, 1770; 6. Sarah,
born April 16, 1772.

Benjamin moved with his family from Haverhill,
Mass., to Concord, N. H., where he became the
owner of valuable real estate. His dwelling-house
was situated at the north end of "The Street."
He carried on his farm and the carpentering
business, and meanwhile opened a tavern in his
house, which he kept for several years, where he
had " an abundance of the County of Coös travel,
the double two-horse sleighs, with their arms set on
end and tackling on, in a large open space in front
of his house, were like ship-masts in a spacious
harbor." His first wife died, at the age of 46
years, Oct. 23, 1777, the same year, as I have
before observed, that my mother, who was her
intimate friend, deceased. He had for his second
wife Ednah Ela,[1] of Haverhill, where they were.

---

[1] It appears from the Haverhill Records, that John Hanna-
ford married, May 5, 1737, Martha Ela; both of Haverhill.
Asa Hannaford married Louis Nichols; both of that town;
their children were : John, born Jan. 20, 1766, Hannah,
William, and Louis. In 1743, fifty-six inhabitants of Haver-
hill signed a petition to "his Excy Wm Shirly Esq Captain
Genl and Gov in Chief over his Majestys province of the
Massachusetts Bay," . . . Among these petitioners were
ZACHARIAH HANNAFORD, Joseph Greely, Nathaniel, Abra-
ham, Lewis, Benjamin, and Ezekiel Page, Samuel, and
Israel Ela, and John Swett.

married Feb. 9, 1779. They became members of the Society of Friends in Concord. In 1789, he was one of a committee, legally chosen by the parish of Concord, to purchase of certain named persons, " all their right and property in a meeting-house [the old North Church] in said Concord, and a lot of land containing one acre and a half." He was an honest, industrious man and a useful citizen of Concord ; at his house a great number of Friends were, from time to time during many years, freely and kindly entertained. He gave an acre and a half of land, lying at the north end of " The Street," to the Weare Monthly Meeting, to be used for a Friends' burial-ground forever. He died May 7, 1811, aged 76 years.

Of PHEBE, the first daughter of Benjamin and Ruth Hannaford, I will relate some incidents, after giving an account of her brother Greely and sisters, Ruth and Sarah.

I have heard Greely relate an anecdote to this effect : His father, soon after moving to Concord, kept open doors for itinerant preachers of the sect of Calvinistic Baptists, and his mother had no ob-jections to it, although at that time she belonged to the Congregational Church in Concord. When about twelve years old, Greely got a little cayenne pepper in his eyes, which of course made them smart. An itinerant Baptist preacher, by the name of Ellen, seeing him thus afflicted, instead of mani-festing any sympathy, laughed at his calamity. A meeting had been appointed to be held on the east side of the Merrimac River, and Ellen was to preach there. When the time arrived to attend it, Greely was told by his father to go and hear brother Ellen preach. " I cannot go," replied Greely, " I do not like him; he laughed at me in my distress, and, besides, I believe that he is a hypocrite." The command was repeated; the boy refused to obey, ran from the house and jumped over the orchard fence. His father in running after him fell flat upon the ground, and, thinking that his fall proved Greely's opinion of Ellen to be correct, gave up the pursuit and never again asked his son to hear the preaching of Calvinistic Baptists.

Greely learned carpentering of his father, and, at the age of about twenty-one years, went to Portland, Me., where he established himself in business, and, in the course of a number of years, built many dwelling-houses, stores, and sea-going vessels; he also engaged in commercial pursuits, and thus lost property by the French cruisers on the ocean. He was twice married, first to Mary Webb, who died soon after his pecuniary losses, and afterward to Miriam Stickney.

It is said that " truth lies deep in the bottom of a well." Our aim should be to seek for truth in all matters. A minister of the Society of Friends, whom I heard preach in Lynn, Mass., sixteen years ago, remarked, that " Religion is a thing, which, rightly understood and practised, makes men wiser and better." Greely Hannaford sought for truth amidst several popular religious sects, but finally, as he believed, found it while at "a despised Quakers' Meeting." [1] He joined the Society of

---

[1] A person who had never attended a religious meeting of Friends, and was unacquainted with their doctrines and customs, would, on going into their meeting-house, while they were assembled for worship, look in vain for a minister's pulpit, a choir of singers, or a musical instrument of any kind. "Is it fancy or not," said a Presbyterian writer, after attending a Friends' Meeting, "that Friends go into their meeting-houses with a more natural, unaffected air than worshippers into temples of more pretension? Is there a sort of formal pace for our carpeted aisles, as if the organ voluntary, like a military tune, demanded a movement of its own? I hardly know. Hark! some one speaks. It is one of the female elders beneath the narrow windows. 'They who wait upon the Lord shall renew their strength; they shall mount up with wings of eagles; they shall run, and not be weary; they shall walk, and not faint.' She says nothing more. . . . The first day that William Penn, a gentlemanly, courtly, spirited young fellow, went with his college companions to hear Thos. Loe, the Quaker itinerant, as they called him, preach in Oxford, what a glorious day that was for Pennsylvania, — for the whole world!"

"Reader," says Charles Lamb, "would'st thou know what true peace and quiet mean; would'st thou find a refuge from the noises and clamors of the multitude; would'st thou enjoy at once solitude and society; would'st thou possess the depth of thine own spirit in stillness, without being shut out from the consolatory faces of thy species; would'st thou be alone, and yet accompanied; solitary, yet not desolate; singular, yet not without some to keep thee in countenance; a unit in aggregate; a simple in composite:—come with me into a

Friends and, after a while, was by them appointed one of their ministers. He[1] purchased a farm,

Quakers' Meeting. Dost thou love silence deep as that 'before the winds were made?' Go not out into the wilderness; descend not into the profundities of the earth; shut not up thy casements; nor pour wax into the little cells of thy ears, with little-faith'd self-mistrusting Ulysses. Retire with me into a Quakers' Meeting. For a man to refrain even from good words, and to hold his peace, it is commendable; but for a multitude it is great mastery. . . . More frequently the Meeting is broken up without a word having been spoken. But the mind has been fed. You go away with a sermon not made with hands. O when the spirit is sore fretted, even tired to sickness of the janglings and nonsense-noises of the world, what a balm and a solace it is, to go and seat yourself, for a quiet half hour, upon some undisputed corner of a bench, among the gentle Quakers. . . . The very garments of a Quaker seem incapable of receiving a soil; and cleanliness in them to be something more than the absence of its contrary. Every Quakeress is a lily."

But how is a Friends' Meeting broken up? One of the elders, it may be, stands up; he shakes hands with another; then others shake hands; the quiet assembly begins to go away. The Meeting is done.

[1] In 1839 he published a pamphlet, written in an odd style, entitled, "The Herald of the Glorious Morning of Emmanuel, and Genius of Universal Emancipation," from which the following are extracts: —

" I served as an apprentice, under my father's instruction, at the joiners' business, until I was about twenty years old, when he set me free for I had far exceeded him in workmanship. Some months afterward I moved to Portland, Me., where I built ships, brigs, and sloops, prospered exceedingly and married Mary Webb, a very amiable woman, who was a help-mate indeed. I laid up earthly treasures in abundance

dwelling-house, and other buildings, situated a few miles from Portland, on Cape Elizabeth, moved there with his family, and died in 1851, aged about 84 years.

until the French spoliation, which swept off all my personal property, and, in addition to this loss, my wife died. This was a trying time to me, and I could say, in the language of Micah, 'Ye have taken away my gods, and what have I more?' I knew not the true God and was in great trouble. . . . My demand on our Government, on account of the French spoliations, is more than nine thousand dollars. . . . After a while the Lord opened the way for me to prosper again in business, and I married Miriam Stickney who stood high in the ranks of female virtue. By my two wives I had seven sons and two daughters. My heavenly Father visited me in various ways. My prayer to Him day and night was for wisdom to enable me to walk worthily in the path of duty; meantime I went to the many 'lo-heres and lo-theres,' like millions of my fellow-beings, to find the Saviour of Life in mankind. At last, I went to a Quakers' Meeting, there being one held in Portland, but heard no preaching; thinking that they had preaching sometimes, I went once more to one of these Meetings, sat on a back seat, and, after a considerable length of time, a woman stood up and spoke so appropriately to my state of mind, that I was astonished, and, like Paul, struck down to the ground at noon-day. After attending the meetings many times, I had a gift in the ministry that stands in the unchangeable priesthood, was nominated by the Monthly and Quarterly Meetings of Friends, my name sent up to the Yearly Meeting at Newport, R. I., and I was appointed a minister in unity with them.

. . . "If Martin Van Buren is governed by the wisdom of the just and rules in righteousness, . . . would be expelled from Congress, for they shed my friend Cilley's blood, leaving his excellent wife and four children to mourn their loss."

Ruth, the second daughter of Benjamin and Ruth Hannaford, married Bela Turner, by whom she had three children, one dying in infancy. The two remaining were named Lucy, and John H. Lucy, born Dec. 7, 1792, at Hanover, N. H., married Nicholas Jones, by whom she had one son, Benjamin H.[1] She died Feb. 3, 1816, aged 23 years, 1 month, and 26 days. John H., born Sept. 19, 1794, died Oct. 19, 1796.

A short time after her brother Greely joined the Society of Friends, Ruth went to Portland, where she remained a while at his house. He explained to her the doctrines of Friends, and the result was that she became convinced of their truth, joined the Society and afterward returned to Concord where she promulgated these doctrines, being the first person who generally introduced them in the town, and caused a Meeting of Friends to be established there. For several years past, she[2] has lived in Lynn, Mass.

Sarah, the third daughter of Benjamin and Ruth Hannaford, married, April 4, 1792, Moses Swett, (an officer in the United States navy,) by whom she had six children, as follows: 1. Sally; 2. Frederic W.; 3. Mary Eastman, who was born July 13, 1796, and married, Oct. 27, 1819, Nathan

---

[1] He, together with his father and mother, was a member of the Society of Friends, of which he became a Minister.

[2] She died Sept. 18, 1854, aged 84 years, 2 months, and 27 days.

Breed,[1] of Lynn, Mass.; he was born in 1794; 4. Benjamin H.; he was born in 1798, and married his cousin Mehitable Swett, in 1823; the names of their children are, Lucy T., Sarah Frances, Ann Maria, and James Edward; 5. Ednah H., and Abraham; the last two were twins.

Sarah joined the Society of Friends a number of years after marrying Moses Swett, who died in 1819; in 1822 she married a worthy member of this Society, James Breed,[2] of Lynn, Mass., a widower, who, by his first wife, was the father of Nathan Breed, who married Sarah's daughter, Mary E.[3]

---

[1] They are members of the Society of Friends; their children were as follows: 1. Moses S., who married Deborah P. Phillips; 2. Sarah S., who married Alfred Hacker; 3. Lucy J., now deceased, who married Henry M. Hacker; 4. Mary S., who married William Bradford; 5 and 6. James E., and Hannah E., twins; 7. Catharine, who, two years after Lucy J's death, married Henry M. Hacker.

[2] He died Sept. 18, 1848, aged 89 years.

[3] Her mother died Dec. 15, 1863, aged 92 years, 7 months, and 29 days. A short time before dying she said, "This is mortal putting on immortality." Her goodness is associated with my remembrances from early childhood up to the present moment. She was indeed a good Christian; lovely and noble traits were hers, self-sacrificing, true, and kind; but now

> " The golden bowl is broken,
> The silver chord undone;
> And a pilgrim, worn and weary,
> To her long, long home is gone."

CHAPTER VI.

MY MARRIAGE TO PHEBE HANNAFORD. — ACCOUNT OF OUR CHILDREN, THEIR BIRTHS, MARRIAGES, ETC. — OUR CONNECTION WITH THE PRESBYTERIAN CHURCH. — WITH THE SOCIETY OF FRIENDS.

ON February 23d, 1789, I married PHEBE, daughter of Benjamin and Ruth Hannaford. We had six daughters and four sons, namely: Ruth, Anna, Harriet, Mary, Lucy Lund, John, William, Ednah Hannaford, and Samuel; our tenth child died in infancy.

My daughter Ruth was born Dec. 29, 1789. Sixty-four years have passed since her birth, and goodness has ever been prominently manifested in all her actions. During her earlier years, while I associated with people who were fond of dancing, fashionable apparel,[1] and various other things that King Solomon pronounced *vanity*, she was allowed to attend, for several weeks, a dancing-school at Exeter, N. H., and after returning home danced, at my request, while I played lively tunes on my

---

[1] On certain occasions, for some time before and after his marriage, my father wore a very handsome suit of scarlet-colored cloth.

bass-viol. At length, becoming a member of the Society of Friends, she renounced such gay amusements ; she qualified herself for school teaching, and afterward pursued this occupation for some time.

A young man, by the name of Daniel Cooledge,[1]

[1] This surname has been, at different periods of time, spelt thus : Coalyng, Couling, Cullinge, Colynge, Cullidge, Coledge, Cowlidge, Cooledge, Coolidge, &c. As " a desire to trace a lineage and to perpetuate its remembrance," has been prevalent among mankind in all ages, the following genealogical account is here inserted. In Dr. H. Bond's " Genealogies," &c., may be seen " Pedigrees of Cooledges in Cambridgeshire, England," furnished by Mr. H. G. Somerby, who says, the name, Coalyng, first appears in the Subsidy Rolls for 1327, where Walter and Ralph Coalyng were assessed for lands in Wimpole, in Cambridgeshire. In the time of Henry VIII., the family were seated in Arrington, and, judging from the Wills, were at that time of wealth and great respectability, belonging to the gentry."

The following are extracts from Mr. Somerby's explanatory remarks in relation to the pedigrees referred to : —

" It appears in the Rolls of the Hundreds, time of Edward the First, that William de Coulinge held lands in Cambridgeshire, from which one can reasonably infer that the family was then seated in that County. Many families of Saxon origin copied the example of their Norman conquerors, and prefixed *de* to their names; . . . generally speaking it was dropped from surnames about the time of Henry the Sixth. Thus, instead of William de Coulinge, &c., the landed gentry wrote themselves William Coulinge of Coulinge. In Burke's " Dictionary of Arms " are several varieties in the spelling of the name, evidently of one common origin, from the similarity of the arms."

born Jan. 18, 1785, in Bolton, Mass., having
served an apprenticeship at bookbinding, and belonging to the Society of Friends, established himself in Concord, N. H., in the year 1807, as a
bookseller and binder, on Main Street, near the
place where I commenced the business of clock-
making. Soon after his settlement in business, he
formed the acquaintance of my daughter Ruth, and
the marriage compact was concluded between them

The Cooledges or Coolidges of this country, are believed
to be directly descended from William de Coulinge, before
mentioned. The name of the first Cooledge who came from
England to Dorchester, Mass., was Philip; he had a son,
Philip, who married a daughter of Captain Piper, of Acton,
Mass., and afterward settled in Newburyport. A son by this
marriage, named Philip, settled in Bolton, Mass., where he
married into the Fosdike family, and by his wife had several
children, two of whom were named Sarah, and William; the
latter with his father, became identified with the patriot cause
in the Revolutionary War. They fought at Lexington, Concord, and Bunker Hill, and served under Washington on the
Hudson, for a while, then returned to their homes, Philip to
Bolton, and William to Philipston, where he married Phebe
Shattuck, who subsequently died; he afterward moved to Bolton and married again, and was the founder of the Baptist
Society of that town. He died in Bolton, March 15, 1826,
aged 72 years; he was the father of the Daniel Cooledge,
mentioned in the text, and also of a daughter named Lydia,
who married Elijah Dunton, by whom she had a number of
children. This last-mentioned family moved to Westport, on
Lake Champlain, New York, where the husband died, and
sometime afterward the widow went with her family to Cambridge, Vt., where she died in the year 1848.

April 29, 1812.[1]   They had three children, namely :
Phebe Hutchins, George Fox, and William Penn ;
of whom the following is an account : —

1. Phebe Hutchins, who was born Feb. 17,
1814, and named for my wife, has now arrived at
the age of about 39 years, I being 53 years old at
the time of her birth.   She belongs to the Society
of Friends, and manifests in her many kind acts noble qualities of mind and heart ; she married Francis
Metford, now deceased, by whom she had one
daughter, named Elizabeth ; 2. George Fox, born
Oct. 6, 1815, named for the founder of the Society
of Friends, is unmarried ; 3. William Penn, born
Aug. 25, 1817, married Susan Knapp,[2] Dec. 16,
1850.   He was named for the well known early
Friend,[3] the founder of Pennsylvania.

[1] The following notice, respecting this marriage, was published in one of the Concord, N. H., newspapers : —

> " ' Happy the youth that finds the bride
>   Whose birth is to his own allied. '

"Married, at the Friends' North Meeting-House, in Weare,
N. H., on the 29th ult., [April 29, 1812,] Daniel Cooledge,
bookseller, of this [Main] Village, to Ruth Hutchins, of the
West Parish Village of this town."

[2] Their children are : Ada, born Nov. 28, 1852 ; Florence,
born Jan. 28, 1856 ; Leila, born Sept. 4, 1857.

[3] "In 1681, the celebrated WILLIAM PENN obtained of
Charles II. a grant of the tract of country afterward named
from him *Pennsylvania*.   It was granted to him in consideration of debts due from the crown of England for services
performed by his father, Admiral Penn.   In 1682, he arrived
in the country, accompanied by about 2000 associates, who
were, most of them, like himself, of the denomination of

My son-in-law, Daniel Cooledge, after continuing his business, at the place before mentioned, a number of years, erected a building for his shop and store, a short distance below, on Main Street, near his dwelling-house. To this building he then transferred his entire business, which he carried on prosperously for several years. He informed me of his having at one time a contract with Messrs. Lincoln and Edmunds, booksellers of Boston, to bind *sixty thousand* duodecimo school Bibles, of which I think he completed *forty thousand.* This would be considered, even in these days, a matter of considerable magnitude. He taught a number of young men the art of bookbinding, among whom were Samuel and Charles Wells. The former having served his apprenticeship, devoted his time principally to literary pursuits; after a while he practised law, and at length became a Judge in one of the Courts of the State of Maine.[1]

The years following the war of 1812–15 were not the most prosperous or favorable to business-men, especially the famine year 1816, and my son-in-law experienced, in common with many engaged in mercantile pursuits, such signal defeats in his

Friends or Quakers; and in the next year he laid out the plan of the City of Philadelphia. This great man and wise legislator made civil and religious liberty the basis of all his institutions." — *Elements of History,* &c.

[1] On March 4th, 1856, Judge Wells was inaugurated Governor of that State for one year.

business plans, as to become at length seriously
embarrassed. Being extremely conscientious, and
making it a principle to render to all men their
just due, the fear of insolvency deprived him of the
hope and courage necessary to battle with misfor-
tune. He resolved to make an assignment of his
property for the equal benefit of his creditors, and
to try in a new field to repair his shattered fortunes.
He therefore set out for New York, where he
arrived January 1, 1821, and soon obtained employment of one of his creditors in that city, Messrs.
Samuel Wood and Sons; who gave him charge of
the bookbindery connected with their bookstore,
No. 261 Pearl Street. His family followed him
in, May, 1821.

He remained with his employers for three years
and a quarter, and in May, 1824, commenced business on his own account at No. 66 Fulton, near
Gold Street. He continued to carry on the same
business, in various localities, until 1833, when he
set up the bookselling business at No. 323 Pearl
Street, Franklin Square, for the benefit of himself
and his sons. Here he continued with various results until February, 1838, when, losing heart by
reason of the many troubles which beset business
men in those perilous times, he made a second
assignment, and did not enter into business again.

Although thus unfortunate in his business expe-
riences, no debt of his contracting, either of principal or interest, ever went unpaid. In settling his

estate in Concord, there was a deficiency of only
$500 due to various persons.   This was paid out of
the first earnings of himself and family, in New
York, his employers there having, at his request,
deducted weekly from his salary a sum to apply on
the $205 due them, as a part of the deficiency
mentioned, and it was fully liquidated mostly in this
way.[1]   His second assignment had the same issue.
In May, 1839, his assignees settled his estate by
paying his debts in full, principal and interest, except to one creditor, who refused the *interest*, and
the surplus assets were left in the hands of his sons.
He had taught them his trade of bookbinding, that
the knowledge thus gained might serve as a re-
source in case of possible future necessity ; and they
also gained some knowledge of the business of bookselling and publishing.   His principle, that " a debt
is a debt until it is paid," thus had, in his own case,
due illustration.

His sons continued the business on their own account, first, near, and afterward opposite the place
where he began bookselling in 1833, — that is, in

---

[1] When he got all the receipts together, he wrote on the
package containing them : " Thankful for favors from on
high."   The following is his autograph : —

Pearl Street, Franklin Square. From this small beginning theirs has grown to be a prominent book establishment, their business being the manufacture and sale of blank, school, and other books, among which is the well-known "Webster's Elementary Spelling Book."[1] When I have been in New York, at their place of business, I have seen great numbers of this Spelling Book in the process of packing for shipment, mostly to the South and Southwest, and they have told me that their sales were counted by *millions!* Truly, they may say with King Solomon, "to the making of many books there is no end."

My son-in-law, Daniel Cooledge, the year after giving up business, as before detailed, suffered an attack of paralysis of the left side, and though his life was lengthened out several years, yet he continued to be an invalid to the end of his days.

---

[1] They published this book under license direct from Noah Webster, the author, and owner of the copyright, for some years before his death, in 1843, and after that event they purchased the residue of the term of the copyright, about thirteen and a half years, from his executors, Messrs. White and Ellsworth, for eighteen thousand dollars. They published in that time, ending May, 1857, no less than 12,361,075 copies, worth, at the wholesale price of six cents, about *seven hundred and fifty thousand dollars.* After their interest in it ceased, the family of Dr. Webster took the needful steps for a fourteen years' extension of the copyright, and it is now published by a New York House. The sales of late years have, however, especially since the Rebellion, been greatly curtailed.

He died at his son George's house in New York, Nov. 1, 1847, aged 62 years, 9 months, and 13 days. His [1] remains were interred in the Friends' burial-ground in Houston Street, near the Bowery.

He was an honest, intelligent man, and his devotion to religion was refined by his faith and love toward God. He was grave in speech and action, noble in demeanor, remarkably particular in having all things, over which he had control, tidy and in good order, inclined to moderation in all things, and of an equable temper. Books of a moral or religious tone, that he believed would be beneficial for his fellow-beings to read, he published and distributed gratuitously. He regarded man's existence on earth as being wisely instituted by Providence, and devoutly believed that mankind, by pursuing THE STRAIGHT PATH, would be fully rewarded by the Deity here and hereafter. I have seen pasted on the wall of the room, in front of his usual place while engaged at bookbinding, various passages that

[1] He passed the last years of his life in contentment and peace. In a letter, that he wrote a few days before his death, he quoted from Dr. Watts these words : —

" Thy food and raiment,
House and home thy friends provide,
And without thy care or payment,
All thy wants are well supplied."

In 1863, his remains were removed from the Houston Street burial-ground to the Friends' Cemetery on Long Island. See *note*, page 99.

he had copied from books; among them were the
following lines : —

> "How shocking must thy summons be, O Death!
> To him that is at ease in his possessions!
> Who, counting on long years of pleasure here,
> Is quite unfurnished for the world to come!"
>
> *Young.*

A man once said to him, " In number, the Quakers
are very few indeed in New York." He replied,
" By those few the City may be preserved from
destruction." While conversing with a friend of
mine, Daniel remarked, " Every man should have
noble aims in view." His widow still holds fast to
the good old " Quaker " doctrines, and enjoys many
blessings in the kind attentions and manifold acts of
her [1] children.

[1] She died at her son George's house, in the City of New
York, on Sunday morning, at seven o'clock, Sept. 6, 1863,
aged 73 years, 8 months, and 7 days. She attended the
Friends' Meeting, on the Sunday preceding that of her
death, and took a cold, to which was added another on Tues-
day following. The next day she was attacked with pleurisy,
complicated with inflammation of the lungs, failed rapidly in
strength, and experienced severe bodily pains until near
the hour when she was removed from the earth to a better
world. Her remains and her husband's now lie buried in the
rural cemetery belonging to the Friends, five miles from the
City, on Long Island.

Of the spot containing the remains of RUTH COOLEDGE,
it may justly be said, that "no holier dust through all her
zones hath earth in keeping." She indeed " held fast to the
pure religious principles of the early Friends," and was im-
bued with celestial qualities of mind and heart, — being kind,

The following is an extract from a letter, written by Judge Waterman, of New York, to William P.,

affectionate, ever ready and willing to comfort the distressed, cheerful in affliction, wise in conduct and counsel, diligent in well-doing, firm in the belief of the immortality of the soul, and loving towards God and his Son, Jesus Christ. Most truly it may be said of her, that she was PURE IN HEART. "Blessed are the pure in heart for they shall SEE God." Most truly, too, it may be affirmed of her, that she was a PEACE-MAKER. "Blessed are the peace-makers for they shall be called the children of God." She really rejoiced in goodness wherever it was found. "Rejoice and be exceeding glad for great is your reward in heaven." Ever faithful in the performance of the duties of life, time with her passed well employed. Believing that "God is a shield to them that put their trust in him," she did not fail to seek, lean on, and obey him with her WHOLE HEART. "Blessed are they that keep his testimonies, and that seek him with their whole heart. They also do no iniquity; they walk in his ways." The morning came — the holy Sabbath morn — when her soul left its earthly tabernacle. She was prepared to see this morn, and, before seeing it, could devoutly say, —

"Rise, happy morn! rise, holy morn!
Draw forth the cheerful day from night:
O Father! touch the east, and light
The light that shone when Hope was born."

Her soul passed onward. It seemed as if "the hand of Almighty God certainly had raised in her soul such unbounded adoration and love, that her only object was, to be worthy to appear before the presence of such excellent goodness, and partake of the joys of heaven." At length, —

"The golden bowl was broken,
And the silver chords unstrung,

son of Daniel Cooledge, some time after the decease of the latter : —

. . . "I can hardly express to you how much I valued your father's [1] friendship, or the influence his example exerted on me. In all his life he seemed to recognize, that 'Order was Heaven's first law.' In business he was severely methodical; in dress critically neat; in social intercourse unpretendingly kind, conferring a favor in seeming unconsciousness; and in administering a rebuke, he did it plainly and directly, without the least pharisaical assumption.

"The last time I saw him in life, I met him in the Park, near the City Hall. I saw at once that he moved with a halting step, and was pained to hear that he was suffering from an attack of paral-

> Ere our hearts received a token
> Of the grief that o'er us hung.

> "She is not dead! The earthy
> Only sleepeth with the earth;
> The precious spirit lives in all
> Its pure undying worth."

[1] In 1834, he published, for gratuitous distribution, a little book, a copy of which he gave to Judge Waterman, entitled, "The Young Man's Pocket Companion," containing George Washington's Farewell Address, the Declaration of Independence, the Constitution of the United States, etc.

"The only safe and lasting foundation for a Republican Government to be based upon must be intelligence, virtue, and the religion of Jesus Christ.

"'Whatsoever ye would that men should do unto you, do ye even so unto them.' — *Bible.*"

ysis.   He viewed the event, he remarked, as a pre-
monition that his summons to die would be sudden,
and might come at any moment.   ' I have endeav-
ored to prepare for the chance of being overtaken
in the street,' he said, ' by wearing this slip of paper in my hat,' taking it off at the same time, and
showing his name and address attached to the lining.
His conversation, at this interview, satisfied me that
he was living in constant expectation of, and preparation for, death.   He spoke to me solemnly of the
importance of living near to God, and of being
prepared to die.   On hearing of his death, I[1] felt

1 The following is a copy of a letter that he wrote to George
F. Cooledge, on his [George's] mother's death, and the extract subjoined is taken from a letter that he wrote to William, on the same occasion : —

"*New York, Sept. 9, 1863.*

"GEO. F. COOLEDGE : My friend, — I yesterday looked
my last on what remained of your now sainted mother.   She
will return to us no more ; but, my friend, let us who remain
on earth so live that we may go to her.   She was one of God's
people, sought to do good to all, and evil to none.   She was
your best earthly friend.   May the Redeemer, whom she
loved and served in life, sustain you in your bereavement.

"I know your loss for I had a mother once like yours ; she
was a devoted mother, but she, too, is dead.   I am left as you
are left by your mother's death, — parentless.   Alas ! I have
recently lost my wife, and I am childless.   Both of us, then,
are fatherless, motherless, wifeless, and childless.   I realize
that we have many bonds of sympathy in the similarity of our
causes of sorrow.   God be with you, my esteemed friend, and
sanctify this affliction to you in giving you a closer walk with
Him.   As to your mother, she is happy now.   Her life below
affords us that assurance.

that I had lost a life-long friend, and society an honest, useful, and Christian member."

> " No sickness, nor sorrow, or pain
>   Shall ever disquiet her now,
> For death to her spirit was gain,
>   Since Christ was her life when below.

> " Her soul has now taken its flight
>   To mansions of glory above,
> To mingle with angels of light,
>   And dwell in the kingdom of love.

" In life I counted your father and your mother among my early and best friends; from whom, when I was young and a stranger in this great City, I experienced nothing save kindness. Their memory will be cherished by me while I live, and I pray that I may join them and their children in heaven.

" Your sincere friend,   WM. D. WATERMAN."

. . . " I am thankful to have been permitted to enjoy your mother's acquaintance and friendship. In 1830, while a student at law, in this City, on the recommendation of the Rev. Cyrus Mason of the Presbyterian Church, in Cedar Street, I became a member of your father's family, and thus acquainted with your mother. This acquaintance ripened into sincere and grateful friendship; for young and a stranger in the City, she gave me sympathy and encouragement; I felt that she was my friend. If I have ever known a truly Christian woman, such an one I knew in your departed mother. I think I never knew a character so faultless, so full of kindness, charity, peace, and good-will to all the world. During the period of our long acquaintance, I never saw her in anger, never heard her utter a hasty or inconsiderate word, and never heard her speak in disparagement of any person; if she could truthfully utter nothing in praise, she was silent. I shall cherish her memory as having been one of the most nearly perfect human characters that I ever knew.

" Your friend,   WM. D. WATERMAN."

My daughter Anna, born Aug. 29, 1791, lives, as I have before observed, at our old homestead in West Concord. She deserves, and will surely receive, the reward of " Well done, thou good and faithful woman."

My daughter Harriet, born May 13, 1793, was married Sept. 15, 1819, to Daniel, son of Thomas Holder,[1] of Berlin, Mass. Daniel was born May 19, 1791, in Berlin, was a member of the Society of Friends, became the owner and cultivator of a good farm in that town, and his[2] dwelling-house and other buildings were situated on the same. Their children were: 1. Maria,[3] born June 28, 1820; 2. Samuel H., born Aug. 26, 1821, died April 24, 1822; 3. Samuel, born March 2, 1823, married, March 22, 1842, Louisa M. Price, of Marlborough, Mass.; their children were: Charles

---

[1] He was born on the island of Nantucket, and married Sarah Gaskill, of Mendon. He died February, 1830, aged 75 years; she died Nov. 6, 1836, aged 77 years. Their children were: 1. Phebe, who married Silas Cooledge; she died November, 1832; 2. Hannah, who died April 20, 1848, aged 66 years; 3. Joseph, who married three times; 4. David, who married Ruth Bassett; 5. DANIEL, of whom an account is given in the text and a subsequent note; 6. Thomas, who married Lucy Fosgate; he died Oct., 1856, aged 63 years; 7. John, who married Caroline A. Russell; he died Feb. 6, 1864, aged 64 years.

[2] He died May 18, 1863, aged 71 years, 11 months, and 29 days.

[3] She died Sept. 18, 1863, aged 42 years, 11 months, and 20 days.

Edward,[1] Lambeth Bigelow, Lyman Daniel, and
Emily Lucinda ; 4. Phebe,[2] born Nov. 27, 1824 ;

[1] He enlisted in the 13th Massachusetts Regiment as a
drummer.

[2] She wrote me an account of the death of her father and
sister Maria, from which I extract as follows : —

. . . "Last autumn, my father began to complain of weari-
ness and a bad feeling about his heart. . . . On Monday,
[May 18, 1863,] he rose at five in the morning, and when
I looked from the chamber window, soon after, I saw him
destroying caterpillars' nests upon his trees. He ate breakfast with us as usual. . . . At noon I went to the cornfield ;
he had not been there. While I was returning to the house,
my sister Maria came to me, saying, ' A boy had just stopped
at the house and told us that our father is lying on the ground
near the pasture bars !' . . . I saw the lifeless form of my
dear father upon the ground ! . . . After the body was laid
out in the bedroom, Jane and I sat by its side, and a beautiful
bird, on a tree close by the window, poured forth a song of
the richest melody. Mary and I with Jane and her husband
rode over to the new cemetery, in Berlin, near the close of
the day, and, as the sun was setting, we entered the holy and
beautiful burial-place, while the bell told the years of our
father's life, — SEVENTY-TWO. We stood together in hushed
silence and listened ! The funeral was on Wednesday, the
20th, at 10 o'clock, A. M. . . . The day was perfect ; the air
soft and balmy, laden with the perfume of apple blossoms.
The glad sunshine looked into the open grave and rested
upon the coffin of our beloved father. And so we left him
in the quiet grave. . . .

"But yet four short months from the very day father died,
and the shadowy death presence was again in our stricken
household. We stood by the bed of our dying sister Maria.
. . . And so another grave was made in our holy burial-place.
' In the cold, moist earth we laid her when the forest cast its

she graduated at the Westfield State Normal School, and is now a teacher; 5. Jane, born July 30, 1827, married, June 12, 1851, Charles Bigelow, of Marlborough, where they now live; their children are: Charles Herbert, Edward Daniel, and Alfred Putnam; 6. Mary H., born July 8, 1823, graduated at the Westfield State Normal School, and is now a teacher; 7. Levi,[1] born Aug. 17, 1837.

My daughter Mary was born July 13, 1795. While on a visit at New York City, in 1821, she became acquainted with Peter Worden, who belonged to the Society of Friends. He made proposals of marriage to her, and wrote to my wife and me for our approval of the same; our reply being satisfactory to him, they were married April 24, 1822. Shortly afterward they came to Concord, where he taught a private school in the Main Village.[2] His memory was extraordinary, man-

leaf.' But we have laid the precious dust there in a sure and certain hope of a resurrection unto life eternal. But a little while and we too shall go. If our life-work is WELL DONE it matters not how soon. We have reared the last tribute of love, — the snowy marble over the sacred spot where our dear ones lie. On the one is written, —

"DEAR FATHER.

"'HE GIVETH HIS BELOVED SLEEP.'

" On the other, —

"'HER END WAS PEACE.'"

[1] He enlisted in the 27th Massachusetts Regiment as a *fifer*, was in the Burnside expedition, and taken prisoner.

[2] Before opening the school, he was examined in various branches of knowledge, by a learned School Committee, an-

ners prepossessing, and moral and religious conduct unexceptionable; his morning and evening prayers I often heard while he and his wife passed several weeks at my house. A religious meeting of his appointment, in which he delivered an extemporaneous discourse, was held in the school-house of this (West Concord) village, and he gave utterance to these words: "If Baal be God serve him; religion, pure and undefiled, is what we all need. As a tree falls so it lies, and as we live so we shall die." They had by this marriage one child, a daughter, named Antoinette. From Concord, accompanied by his wife, he went to Virginia and there died. Soon after this event she returned to my house, and was a member of my family until her decease, March 1, 1832, aged 36 years, 7 months, and 18 days. Through life she was kind and generous to all around her, and performed well her part in all things. Her daughter, Antoinette, married Gilbert Perkins, of Gloucester, Mass., by whom she has had several children; one of them was named Levi, and another Ella.

My daughter Lucy Lund was born April 8, 1797; I gave her this name as a token of respect to my father's second wife, Lucy Lund. There is no remissness in my daughter Lucy's performance

swered their questions readily and correctly, and received a certificate of recommendation, &c. In turn he asked the Committee mathematical and other questions, which, though easily solved by himself, his interrogators could not rightly answer.

of good deeds, and she is remarkable for her industrious habits. All of my children, as they grew in years, displayed this good quality, fully realizing the importance of improving time in useful pursuits.

My eldest son, John, was born April 12, 1799. From childhood he showed a capacity for business. When thirteen years old, he had a desire to raise and sell some oats for his own benefit; having obtained my permission, he sowed the seed, undoubtedly entertaining this idea: " You go and bury a seed, but it is done with a view to *reap* a hundred-fold." He was not disappointed in his expectations, for the oats which he harvested, on the acre of land that I appropriated to his use, he sold at a great profit.

Soon after hostilities commenced, in 1812, between the United States and Great Britain, a Company of United States troops, on their march to the Canadian frontier, halted a while in this (West Concord) village. The Captain of the Company came to me and inquired whether I would let him have a wagon with two horses, and a boy to drive, at a fair price, to go a distance of about 20 miles on the march? I replied "Yes." My son John, with the team, accompanied the soldiers. As he did not return at the time specified, I feared that he had been enticed to go even to the seat of war, and therefore hastened in pursuit, but met him on his way back, well pleased with the adventure.

His next important business was to sell books for

Daniel Cooledge, by taking them in a wagon around the country. After devoting two months to this business, he tended store a while, in this village, for Francis N. Fisk; but desiring to be employed elsewhere, he went to Lynn, Mass., and there learned to make ladies' shoes of a man to whom he bound himself by indenture to serve as an apprentice for a number of years. But he did not continue with this man during the full period of time agreed upon; however, he did not leave without paying him a sum of money for an honorable discharge. So both parties separated from each other by mutual consent. This circumstance reminds me, that Benjamin Franklin, who was an indented apprentice to his brother James, wrote as follows: " My brother was passionate, and had often beaten me, which I took extremely amiss; and, thinking my apprenticeship very tedious, I was continually wishing for some opportunity of *shortening* it, which at length was offered in a manner unexpected," &c.

John having " shortened " his apprenticeship, (and he assigned weighty reasons for so doing,) made preparations for trying his fortune in a southern State. He went to Newbern, N. C., and there officiated as foreman in a shoe establishment. After a while he went to Norfolk, Va., where he obtained employment in another shoe establishment, and finally became a joint owner of it. In the spring of 1830, he moved with his family to the City of New York, where, in the following year, he established himself in a store on the west side of Chatham Square. The "Mammoth Boot," which he placed in front of his store, attracted much notice. He removed his place of business to Broadway, and, subsequently, to the east side of Chatham Square. His dwelling-house was situated in Henry Street. He accumulated a considerable amount of property, and was very highly esteemed by all who knew him as a business-man or otherwise. He was twice married; first, in Norfolk, Va., Aug. 14, 1825, to Julia Ann Lines, who was born in New Haven, Conn., July 11, 1803; by her he had five sons,[1] namely: Augustus, Charles,

---

[1] The following is an account of them: 1. Augustus, born July 8, 1826, was, for a number of years, Secretary of the Boonton, N. J., Iron Works. He died in that town Feb. 23, 1854, aged 27 years, 7 months, and 15 days; 2. Charles, who was born June 26, 1828; on the 7th of February, 1849, he emigrated to the Pacific Coast, and is now living in Idaho Territory; 3. Albert, who was born Aug. 23, 1836; the following year, on July 9th, he met with an accident, while under the care of a black domestic, which immediately caused his death; 4. Another Albert, born Oct. 17, 1832, died Aug. 31, 1833; 5. Alexander, who was born Jan. 22, 1835; he entered Williams College, Mass., in the year 1853, and graduated Aug. 5, 1857, having obtained the highest honors of that institution. He afterward studied Medicine in Boston and New York, and received the Diploma of Doctor of Medicine from the New York Medical College, in March, 1860; also, at the same time, were awarded him the Van Arken Prize, and a Diploma in the Department of Toxicological Chemistry. While in the Medical College, in New York, he was Assistant Editor of the "Journal of Materia Medica,"

Albert, another Albert, and Alexander; the first two were born in Norfolk, Va.; the last three in the City of New York, where she died Nov. 4, 1837, aged 34 years, 3 months, and 23 days. Her remains were carried to New Haven and there buried. He had for his second wife Jane Beebe, a widow, whom he married Sept. 3, 1840; she was born in the City of New York, March 9,

published in that City. On the day after graduating from this College, he was appointed Surgeon of the "Star of the West," in the M. O. Roberts' line of New York, New Orleans, and Havana steamers, and remained in the service for four months, then leaving it to accept the appointment of House Surgeon to the Blackwell's Island Hospitals, and remained on duty in these institutions for a year. In July, 1861, after passing the requisite examinations before the Naval Board, he was commissioned as Surgeon in the regular navy of the United States. After a short service in the Naval Hospital at Brooklyn, and a subsequent service on the United States steamer "Wyandotte," he was ordered to the United States steamer "Harriet Lane," flag-ship of the Potomac Flotilla, remained there till February, 1862, and then detached. After a short leave of absence, he was ordered to the United States steamer "Massachusetts," supply-ship to the Atlantic Squadrons, and remained in her, in charge of medical supplies to the Squadrons, as well as in charge of the sick sent north to hospitals, till July, 1863, when ill health, from hard service, made a resignation necessary. He commenced private practice in De Kalb Avenue, Brooklyn, L. I., September, 1863. On December 16th following, he married Mary F. Pelton, of Poughkeepsie, N. Y.; they have one child, Elizabeth Beecher Hutchins, born Oct. 16, 1864.

1805, and her maiden name was Morrow.   John [1] died in the City of New York June 5, 1843, aged 44 years, 1 month, and 23 days.   His [2] funeral was

1 The following is a copy of a letter I received from him: —

"*New York*, 11*th March*, 1842.

"BROTHER SAMUEL: I feel it my duty, and, by the grace of God, a pleasure to tell you what God has, as I trust, done for my soul, and I give him all the glory for Christ's sake.   I think he has pardoned all my sins, and shed abroad his love in my heart.   I praise him and my prayer to God is, that he will incline you to seek Jesus Christ with all your might.   I pray that you will seek God NOW.   He will forgive all your sins and accept of you for Jesus' sake.   Read the Bible and acquaint yourself with God's promises.   O praise the Lord for his glorious plan of salvation; it is free for all.   O that I had the tongue of an angel, that I might make you know and feel the love of God in Christ.   O turn to the Lord NOW is my prayer for you.   God is merciful and gracious; seek him through Jesus with all your heart, and he will bless you.   My heart burns with love!   Praise the Lord, O my soul!

2 Shortly after his decease I wrote my sister Ruth Cooledge a letter; the following are extracts from hers in reply: —

. . . "I read thy precious letter, and it moved everything within me capable of feeling.   I read it with feelings unutterable; my soul was poured out in prayer and tears before God! . . . Indeed, our brother John has departed from us, and I deeply feel and mourn his loss, but not because I have a doubt that he has gone 'where the wicked cease from troubling, and the weary are at rest.'   Oh! Samuel, how

attended by a large number of persons, who followed his body to the church, in the vault of which it was laid. A short time afterward I brought his remains to Concord, where they were interred in the Friends' burial-ground.

My son William was born Feb. 27, 1801. He also served an apprenticeship at the same trade which his brother John acquired a knowledge of in Lynn. He became a shoe-dealer, first in the City of New York, and afterward in Buffalo, where he married Almira Eldredge, a young lady of much moral worth. He purchased a large lot of land near the outer bound of the City of Buffalo, and was successfully engaged in the shoe business for

much I wished thee could have been a witness, as I was privileged to be, of his sickness and death. For a long time he seemed to have given his heart to God without reserve, and when death approached he was ready to die, as we cannot doubt from the evidence which was manifested to all who were in his chamber and around his dying bed. . . . When he was told that Dr. Watson had no hope of his recovery, *then* he said, 'I am willing to live longer, but not afraid to die; not my will but thine be done, O God!' He seemed to be delighted to know that his mortal life was near to its close, and to feel that he would soon be with Jesus. He prayed to be with him, and implored his wife and me to let him go to Jesus. He took leave of all his children, telling them that he had done all he could for them, and that God will watch over them. His last words were: 'ALL IS PEACE.' . . .

"May the Lord bless thee, Samuel, so hopes and prays thy

affectionate sister Ruth.

about nine years in that city. His health began
to fail in 1836, and he died May 9, 1840, aged 39
years, 2 months, and 12 days. I received from
Elias Greene a friendly letter dated at Buffalo,
May 12, 1840, from which I transcribe as follows:
"I cannot compare your son William's sickness
and death to anything more appropriate than the
burning out of a candle; he seemed to waste away
in the same proportion, and stopped breathing without a single struggle. Your son had the best of
care taken of him by his wife." [1]

[1] My father received from her a letter, from which the
following are extracts: —

. . . "William liked Buffalo the best of any place for
business, but it was his intention and great desire to end his
days in his father's house in Concord. . . . He was confined
to his house about three months before he died. I have the
satisfaction of knowing that he was well taken care of during
his sickness. I took the principal part of the care of him
myself; he did not like to have any one else do anything for
him. . . . He seemed to feel perfectly resigned to the Lord's
will, and said, 'Death has no terrors for me.' For the first
three weeks of his last sickness, he was under great concern
of mind, but by reading the Bible attentively he felt that
peace and happiness which he had not previously enjoyed so
fully; he bore his sickness patiently and without a murmur; he
had little or no pain. During his last three days and nights
he was obliged, on account of his difficulty in breathing, to sit
in a chair, in which he died. He retained his mental powers
to the last moment of his life. We have reason to believe
that he has gone to the bosom of his Saviour. But oh! I am
left to mourn the loss of him — my fondly loved husband."

A poet describes the loss of friends, tenderly beloved, as

My daughter Ednah H., born April 21, 1803, was twice married; first, Dec. 30, 1833, to Greely Hannaford, Jr., her cousin, of Portland, Me., who died Aug. 30, 1853, aged 55 years. In relation to his death she wrote in her Bible the following lines : —

"We should not mourn the loss of friends
  Whom God hath call'd above,
For He, whose kindness never ends,
  Hath taken them in love.

"Now rest in peace, my husband dear;
  Thy earthly toils are o'er;
To loving Jesus thou art near,
  Safe on a heav'nly shore."

On June 14th, 1854, she married Micah Hamer, who was born in Manchester, England; they are pleasantly settled in Lowell, Mass.

Of my son Samuel, who was born Jan. 6, 1806, I will give an account in a subsequent chapter.

In 1790, two young persons, James and Elizabeth Yeats, commenced living in my family. James stayed with us a few years only ; he left very suddenly without giving us any information concerning his intentions. We heard nothing from him till 1817, when he returned to Concord to visit his friends. He then informed us that, during his

follows: "I know well that they who love their friends most tenderly still bear their loss the best. There is in love a consecrated power, that seems to wake only at the touch of death from its repose, in the profoundest depths of thinking souls, superior to the outward signs of grief, sighing, or tears."

absence, he had served in the American Army, fought in a number of battles during the war of 1812–15, married, and settled on a farm in the western part of New Hampshire. His sister Elizabeth continued in my family until a few years before my daughter Ruth was married. Soon after this event she took her abode in Ruth's family, in which she still remains.

Several years after marriage, my wife became impressed with the belief that she ought to join the Presbyterian Church, and that our children should be baptized. Infant baptism had been a subject of discussion between us, she believing in the doctrine, and I entertaining doubts in regard to it, founded on the opinions which I had formed from my study of the Bible, not being able to find authority in the Scriptures for it. Desirous to be enlightened in regard to Christian doctrines, I called one morning at Rev. Asa McFarland's, to make inquiries concerning his views on the subject. He informed me that the "Council of 70" decided that infant baptism was an incumbent duty upon parents; and that accordingly it has been required of those who have signed the "Thirty-nine Articles of Faith," to conform to this decision. His remarks did not have the power to remove the doubts I had entertained. My wife, with three of our children, Ruth, Anna, and Harriet, became members of the Presbyterian Church, and the pastor of which, Rev. Asa McFarland, administered to them the rite of baptism. I did not join this church, but attended its meetings and assisted the choir with my bass-viol.

At length, from the effect of frequent conversations with her sister Ruth, my wife experienced a change in her religious views, but was not hasty in making known, that Christianity, as expounded by George Fox, was more congenial to her mind than that by John Calvin; she desired to walk only in that path of duty which to her plainly appeared to be the right one. I also was convinced that the religious views of Friends well accorded with the precepts taught by Jesus Christ, and was happy to find in them a similarity to my own opinions, especially in regard to infant baptism. After a while my wife communicated her opinions to her Presbyterian associates, and in due time withdrew from their church. Soon after this event we joined the Society of Friends, whose self-denying principles[1] she deemed it her duty strictly to follow. One instance of her regard for these principles

---

[1] A minister of the Society of Friends said, that "A man may think, believe, and rely much upon the sufferings of Christ upon the cross, and at the same time be an utter enemy to the cross of Christ, as it regards his own practical endurance of it, a thing indispensable to a disciple of Christ; and it is very evident that there can be no true follower, without possessing so much of the spirit and power of the cross as will work in him to the mortifying of the deeds of the body, to the sanctifying of the spirit, and to the subjugation of the will of the flesh."

was, that she discontinued wearing certain fashionable articles of dress, though at the time moving in a circle of acquaintances who were ambitious to be arrayed in showy apparel. The plainness of Friends in this respect, and their use of "thee" and "thou," not unfrequently excited the jeers of other Christian denominations. Friends gradually increased in number in Concord, and held their Meetings at Benjamin Hannaford's house, which, after his death, continued to be occupied for several years by his daughters, Ruth and Sarah, and some of their descendants. Abel Houghton, a very worthy man and fluent speaker, frequently expatiated on the subject of religion in these small assemblies. At length, a Meeting-house was built for Concord Friends, and I, having some practical experience in using carpenters' tools, made the seats thereof after the fashion, a very plain one, universally adopted by Friends.[1] In order not to deviate from their

[1] A Friends' Meeting, under the care of, and subordinate to, the Weare Monthly Meeting, was instituted in Concord, N. H., October 24, 1805. In 1814, a Friends' Meeting-House was built in Concord on a lot of land where it stood a number of years. The land was then sold to the Government of New Hampshire, and is now occupied by the State House. The Meeting-House was then moved to the lot given to Friends by Benjamin Hannaford. [See page 83.] In 1840, the Meeting was discontinued, and the house sold to the inhabitants of the school district in which it stood. The heads of families that composed the Meeting were: Ruth Turner, Sarah Swett, Lydia Dunlap, Sarah Arlin, Levi and

plainness in this respect, I went to Weare and took a pattern of the seats in one of the two Friends' meeting-houses situated there.

Phebe Hutchins, Bethiah Ladd, Abel and Sarah Houghton, Daniel and Ruth Cooledge, James and Mary Sanborn, Josiah and Sarah Rogers, Israel and Abigail Hoag, Ruth Hazeltine, and Thomas W. and Ruth G. Thorndike.   Twice every week, for several years, I saw some or all of these Friends assembled in their quiet Meeting, which was sometimes addressed by Josiah Rogers, Sarah Arlin, and two or three others. Formerly, there was much prejudice against the religion of Friends, but

> " The Quaker of the olden time ! —
>   How calm, and firm, and true,
> Unspotted by its wrong and crime,
>   He walked the dark earth through.
> The lust of power, the love of gain,
>   The thousand lures of sin
> Around him, had no power to stain
>   The purity within."
>   *Whittier.*

CHAPTER VII.

A PARTNERSHIP FORMED BY MY BROTHER ABEL AND ME,
IN THE CLOCK-MAKING BUSINESS, IN 1786, AND CONTIN-
UED UNTIL 1807. — MY REMOVAL FROM "THE STREET"
TO WEST PARISH VILLAGE. — ACCOUNTS OF PERSONS,
PLACES, REAL ESTATE, BUSINESS, AND THINGS PERTAIN-
ING TO THIS REMOVAL.

SOON after his marriage, in 1786, my brother
Abel became my partner in the clock-making
business, and our shop stood a little in the rear of
a large, well finished dwelling-house, three stories
high, which we jointly purchased and occupied with
our families, situated in the central part of the
Main Village, on the eastern side of the road or
" Street" before described. Peabody Atkinson and
Jesse Smith were two of our apprentices, and they
eventually established themselves, as farmers, in the
northwestern part of Virginia, where they had
sheep " upon a thousand hills." My brother and
I [1] were successful in our business transactions, and

1 While their father lived in Haverhill they wrote him the
two following letters: —

" *Concord, July 4th*, 1788.

"HONORABLE FATHER: Having an opportunity, by Col.
Kinsman, I write a few lines to you. We are all in good

mutually enjoyed many other blessings. We carried on clock-making together about twenty-one years. Our names may now be seen on the faces of many time-keepers, standing in the corners of sitting-rooms in houses situated in all the New England States; and probably there are eight-day clocks, or timepieces of our manufacture, in all the original thirteen States of the Union. Two eight-day clocks we made to order and sent to the West

health, except my wife, who is as well as we can expect. Yesterday, at nine o'clock, A. M., she gave birth to a fine daughter. [See *ante*, page 63.] My brother Levi has gone to Boston, and intends to get Marm some indigo and tea, which we will send up to you at the first opportunity. I believe we shall buy some land in Concord. Lieut. Bradley will sell us 125 acres, 30 or 40 of which are cleared, containing a young orchard, a house and barn, and situated near Grahame's or Hoyt's, five miles from our house, for $400. Lieut. Bradley will take three clocks, if no more, toward payment for said land, and the remainder in neat stock. My duty to Marm and love to brothers and sisters. From your dutiful son,

Abel Hutchins

" *Concord, Nov.* 12*th,* 1788.

"HONORED SIR: I wish you would call on Esq. Dow, and ascertain what land of Gen. Peabody's is not disposed of, and if you can obtain 200 acres of good land of him, I hope you will write us word immediately. I shall be up to your house at the time of the first sleighing. Please give my love to Marm. Your dutiful son,

Levi Hutchins

Indies.[1] On a part of the land formerly owned by us, immediately in the rear of where our shop stood, is now located a Railroad Passenger Depot, and near it is an extensive Freight Depot. If *John Stevens* could revisit Concord, he would see that many railroads centre at this Depot, namely: the Concord, the Northern, the Boston, Concord and Montreal, the Concord and Claremont, and the Portsmouth and Concord Railroads.

In 1793, my brother Abel and I[2] purchased a farm, situated three miles from this locality, on the western side of Rattlesnake Hill. An honest old gentleman told me that he, when a boy, killed thirteen rattlesnakes one morning, in the month of April, while they were enjoying the warmth of the sun's rays upon a large rock on this hill. Immense

[1] "Their clocks [those manufactured by Levi and Abel Hutchins] were noted as good time-keepers, and are still found in many of the old families. Major Timothy Chandler also manufactured excellent clocks, which are seen now and then among the ancient things." — *History of Concord*, by N. Bouton, D. D.

[2] The following extracts from a letter may interest some of the readers of this book: —

"*Concord, Jan. 9th*, 1793.

"HONORED FATHER: . . . Be kind enough to call in all the grain, that is due to us, immediately, as grain is scarce. I shall be at your house in Rumney soon. If you can get anything of Capt. Wells toward clearing your land, please to inform us by letter, as we expect to sell him a clock. . . . I am in a very great hurry. Your dutiful son,

"LEVI HUTCHINS."

quantities of granite have been quarried on this eminence, which is now called " Granite Hill." Indeed, it affords an inexhaustible supply of this material, which is used for building purposes in Concord, Boston, and other cities of our country. My house is situated near the northern base of this hill, which, besides granite, has produced very many chestnut-trees, and these an abundance of fruit.

Year succeeded year, and time did not pass heavily with my brother and myself. Our aim was to do our duty in all things, and we enjoyed happiness in the reflection that we strove to regard the best interests of our fellow-beings in all our [1] dealings. In the early part of 1807, we dis-

---

[1] The following document shows their kindness to their mother-in-law : —

" KNOW ALL MEN BY THESE PRESENTS: That we, Levi and Abel Hutchins, of Concord, in the County of Rockingham, and State of New Hampshire, Clock-makers, for and in consideration of the sum of One Dollar, together with our natural affection, love, and good will, do demise, grant, and to farm let unto Lucy Hutchins, wife of Colonel Gordon Hutchins, during her natural life, the following articles of Household Furniture, &c., viz.: 1 pair of hand-irons, 1 shovel and one pair of tongs, 1 iron pot, 1 iron kettle, 1 iron teakettle, 1 iron spider, 1 brass warming-pan, 6 common kitchen chairs, 1 large ditto, 1 maple table, 1 pine ditto, 1 desk, 2 trunks, 1 white chest, 1 red ditto, 1 linen wheel, 1 woollen ditto, 1 weaver's loom, 1 large looking-glass, 4 earthen platters, 6 earthen plates, 1 set of cups and saucers, 6 silver teaspoons, 1 block-tin teapot, 1 tea chest, 4 pewter

solved partnership, and, in dividing our property between ourselves, I received the *farm*, which we valued at $1500, as a part of my share; the house, shop, and parcel of land on which they were built, were comprised in Abel's share. All of my children were born in that house, which he continued to occupy until Tuesday, November 25, 1817, when it was consumed by fire.[1] About two years after this event, he erected on its site a first-class hotel, which he conducted for several years.

platters, 1 dozen of pewter plates, 7 tin milk pans, 3 bed-steads, 4 feather beds and bedding to the same, 1 Damask silk gown, 2 chintz gowns, 1 russet gown, 1 red broadcloth cloak, 1 black silk cloak, and 1 camblet riding habit. . . .

"In testimony whereof we have hereunto set our hands and seals, this 24th day of August, 1799.

Levi Hutchins

Abel Hutchins

"Signed, sealed, and delivered in presence of us:—

Moses Swett

John Odlin

[1] Charles Wells, then one of Daniel Cooledge's apprentices, made a correct drawing of the house while the devouring element was raging inside and out of its third story.

In front of it, on a handsome swinging sign, were the words " PHŒNIX HOTEL," and, besides his name, a representation of a phœnix rising amidst flames of fire. After retiring from the management of this hotel, one of his favorite amusements was the cultivation of his garden, where, one year, he raised a musk-melon four feet two inches long! Men are regarded as remarkable when industrious and active at the age of seventy-five years, but these qualities were prominently manifested by him for many years after that period of life.[1]

In 1808, I exchanged with Eben, son of Josiah. Farnum, the hill farm for real estate situated in the then called West Parish, but now West Concord Village, at a distance of about two miles from the north end of " The Street." The principal objects that cheered or depressed the spirits of a traveller along the route between the two villages,

[1] " On the 1st of January, 1819, he [Mr. Abel Hutchins] opened the Phœnix Hotel, which establishment he ever conducted to the entire satisfaction of its guests. In the year 1832, by reason of increasing years, he surrendered his Hotel to his son, Ephraim, and retired to his private dwelling on State Street, where he spent the remainder of his life in tranquillity, cultivating his garden and taking a walk daily, with staff in hand and spectacles on, to the Hotel, for the purpose of meeting old friends, and obtaining the news of the day. Having attached himself to the Whig party, his Hotel became the common boarding-place of the Whig members of the Legislature; but in it all men of all parties and sects received impartial attention and good entertainment." — *History of Concord*, by N. Bouton, D. D.

were a few scattered houses, fertile fields, and
gloomy woods. At two places the road through
the woods was built across deep gullies. Soon
after this exchange of property I moved with my
family to the West Parish Village, which contained
but a few dwelling-houses beside the one that I
had acquired of Eben Farnum, his father having
purchased it of Captain Henry Lovejoy, together
with all the real estate I received in exchange for
the hill farm. This house was two stories high,
and contained four spacious rooms beside the attic.
Contiguous to the house was a part of a *Fort*, built
for protection against the Indians! I soon demolished all that remained of the ancient fortification,
and greatly enlarged the old house.

I have heard Lovejoy tell a story to this effect:
One evening, while riding alone up the road leading from " The Street " to West Parish Village, he
had reason to expect an attack by the Indians.
When arrived at the second gully, a truly fearful
place, he cried out, as if commanding armed men,
"*Follow close after me, my comrades, and be ready
to fire!*" Then making his horse go at full speed,
he reached his home in safety. But real danger
yet awaited him, for he was obliged to go a considerable distance from his house to turn his horse
into pasture. Having accomplished this, he proceeded homeward, but had not gone far when
he discovered that *red men* were near him! He
then secreted himself, and in a short time a num-

ber of Indians [1] passed by near his hiding-place !
The Captain then went home again unharmed.

[1] The seven tribes of Indians, of which the one called *Pennacook* was the most powerful, formerly inhabited the region
of the Merrimac. Passaconaway, who flourished prior to
1670, was a famous Pennacook sagamore or sachem. " Now
hearken to the words of your father," said he. " I am an old
oak that has withstood the storms of more than a hundred
winters. Leaves and branches have been stripped from me
by the winds and frosts ; my eyes are dim ; my limbs totter ;
I must soon fall ! . . . Think, my children of what I say.
These meadows the pale faces shall turn with the plough ;
these forests shall fall by the axe ; the pale faces shall live
upon your hunting-grounds, and make their villages upon
your fishing-places." . . .

" The Bridal of Pennacook" is the title of a poem, by John
Greenleaf Whittier, who, in his notes to it, says : —

" Winnepurkit, otherwise called George, Sachem of Saugus, married a daughter of Passaconaway, the great Pennacook chieftain, in 1662. The wedding took place at Pennacook, (now Concord, N. H.,) and the ceremonies closed with
a great feast. According to the usages of the chiefs, Passaconaway ordered a select number of his men to accompany
the newly married couple to the dwelling of the husband,
where, in turn, there was another great feast. Some time
after, the wife of Winnepurkit expressing a desire to visit
her father's house, was permitted to go accompanied by a
brave escort of her husband's chief men. But when she
wished to return, her father sent a messenger to Saugus, informing her husband, and asking him to come and take her
away. He returned for answer, that he had escorted his wife
to her father's house in a style that became a chief, and that
now if she wished to return, her father must send her back in
the same way. This Passaconaway refused to do, and it is
said that here terminated the connection of his daughter with
the Saugus chief."

The land obtained by me of Eben Farnum, as before mentioned, I will designate as *plain, orchard*, and *building*, the whole embracing about seventy acres. In the course of several years I bought thirty acres more, lying within a mile of the village. The "plain" land, located on the east side of the main road, running through the village, and extending from it to the river and partly permeated by a deep hollow, was in a good state of cultivation, except a few acres of the hollow portion, which were covered with large pine-trees ; these I cut down, often working, with stockings only on my feet, on the sides of the hollow, from daylight till after the dew had dried away in the morning. The "orchard" land, extending from the west side of the main road to the road leading by my house, was in a high state of cultivation, and the many apple-trees growing upon it produced yearly a great deal of fruit. On the land termed "building," was the house[1] and dilapidated fort, a large barn,

[1] Thirty-five years ago I made an attempt at a description of this dwelling-house, &c., as may be seen in the following extracts : —

An old Mansionry, etc.

Upon a gentle, sloping hill,
Near by a busy sawing-mill,
   Stands an ancient mansion ;
And close to it there stood of old,
As oft my father hath me told,
   A FORT for protection.

For Indians there did prowl around,
And raise their war-whoop's awful sound,

wood-shed, and SAW-MILL; the latter being situated, near the dwelling-house, on a BROOK issuing
from LONG POND,[1] which lies in a westerly direction,

> Regardless of their fate;
> Regardless of a Captain bold, —
> Of Captain Lovejoy, as I 'm told, —
>   A man not *small* but " Great."
>
>   .   .   .   .   .
>
> If in this house you go up-stairs,
> You 'll see a room that needs repairs, —
>   Th' " Old Chamber" is its name; —
> But from this room, when fields are green,
> Much that is pleasant may be seen,
>   Though little known to fame.
>
>   .   .   .   .   .
>
> Though " time is ever on the wing,"
> " There is a time for ev'ry thing; "
>   But all things pass away!
> E'en thou, old mansion, soon or late,
> Wilt be remov'd by common fate,
>   When thou hast had thy day.

[1] " Long Pond is a beautiful sheet of water, in the west
part of the town, one mile and three fourths in length, half a
mile in the widest part, and its mean or average width 75¾
rods. As lately surveyed by George Abbot, Esq., it contains
an area of two hundred and sixty-five acres. Its greatest
depth, as measured by Reuben K. Abbot, in the summer of
1852, was eighty-four feet. Fed by streams that gush from
neighboring hills, the water in the Pond is cool, pure, clear as
crystal, and abounds with perch and pickerel, whose color is
bright and sparkling. Only one trout was ever caught in this
Pond; it weighed about five pounds. From the north end
issues a never-failing stream, that affords valuable mill privileges. It is said that no person was ever drowned in this
Pond." — *History of Concord*, by N. Bouton, D. D.

about a mile distant from the mill, and is surrounded by high and low land diversified by trees, farms, and buildings, — the whole scenery affording a very romantic and pleasant appearance. Formerly, this Pond being shallow, a Mr. Flanders undertook to "plough it out," but he was so laughed at and ridiculed that he finally abandoned his foolish enterprise. At the north end, Captain Lovejoy and Josiah Farnum once built a dam, but a more substantial one now occupies its place. The brook, after running a considerable distance near the northern side of Granite Hill, enters my "building" land and soon after is obstructed by a dam, recently rebuilt by myself, where, in 1748, Lovejoy built one, and a shop containing a water-wheel and *Forge* for the manufacture of bar-iron. He obtained the ore from the banks of the Merrimac, just above Concord Bridge; the manufactory was long since demolished, but the name " Forge " was given to the Pond, which still retains it, and a memorial in the form of iron cinders may now be seen near the dam. I caused the new dam to be substantially built for several reasons, one of which is, that it will be the means of saving a great deal of property in the village from destruction, if Long Pond dam should break away. Lovejoy dug a channel, below his dam, for the purpose of conveying the water from the Pond to a place near his house, where the formation of the ground offered a good site for a mill. Josiah Farnum's sons, Josiah,

Eben, and Ephraim, built a grist-mill there, which, after being used a number of years, was taken down; whereupon Eben Duston and a Mr. Howe erected one of these mills on the BROOK, in the village, and used the grinding-stones of the old mill. At length, these mill-stones became the property of the grandfather of NATHANIEL BAKER, ex-governor of New Hampshire, and were carried by the former to a grist-mill which he owned, situated in a village of Concord called " The Borough."

In 1798, subsequent to the time that the mill built by the Farnums was removed, there was built in its place a saw-mill, by John Kimball, of Hopkinton, who sold it to Eben Duston; this was the one standing, as before mentioned, when I moved from " The Street" to West Parish Village. I bought this mill of Duston for $500, and soon after paid William Messer, for repairing it, $300; it was then used a number of years, finally taken down and I replaced it by a new one. A saw-mill has been kept in operation for nearly fifty-five years on this site, and after becoming the owner of one there, I superintended it for eighteen months. At one time, while I was so employed, my son Samuel, who was about five years old, caught his ankle between the cogs of the log-carriage, without much harm. At another time he undertook to help me roll toward the mill a very large log, which, after being started, needed no pushing, on account of the sloping ground; yet he continued to push, and finally went over the log, which rolled over him; but a hollow place in the ground saved him from injury. After the last accident, whenever his mother from the house saw him in or near the mill, she would earnestly beckon with both of her hands to have him come to her.

By the contract between Eben Farnum and myself, respecting our exchange of property, I acquired *the right* of control over the outlet of Long Pond, and exclusively exercised it for more than twenty years. Proximate to the lower or northern side of the dam, a public road crossed, "whereof the memory of man is not to the contrary." I travelled it whenever I pleased, on horseback and otherwise, in 1793 and for many years afterward. It was as much a highway as the one leading by my house, but now it is converted into private uses; for instance, a Mr. —— obtained a quitclaim deed of land, where the road crossed as before mentioned, that gives the control of the Pond gate to the owner of the deed; in this manner the *right* that I acquired of Farnum, and of which he came into possession by way of his father, who obtained it of Captain Lovejoy, to control the outlet of Long Pond, is — *quashed!* The ambition of some men is great, but not always productive of good to their fellow-beings.[1]

[1] "Ambition, in one respect, is like a singer's voice; pitched at too high a key, it comes to nothing. It cares little for persons, — everything for its objects; these it will have at every cost to those." — *C. N. Bovee.*

My ancient friend, Captain Henry Lovejoy, having honestly and industriously fulfilled the duties of his mission on earth, departed this life, in the 90th year of his age, Anno Domini 1805, thirty-one years after my first acquaintance with him. My more modern friend, Eben Farnum, died in 1830. When he moved from West Concord Village, in the spring of 1808, to the house on the hill farm, among the goods and chattels that he carried with him were *sixty barrels of cider*, which he made the preceding autumn ; but he told me that this beverage was all gone before he finished haying the ensuing summer ! [1]

[1] "A man may even be known by the drinks he prefers. Chaste men love light, still wines ; wits and roisterers, sparkling wines ; heavy men, high wines ; and coarse men, malt and spirituous liquors." — *C. N. Bovee.*

CHAPTER VIII.

AN ACCOUNT OF MY SON SAMUEL, ETC.

WHEN sixteen years old, my son Samuel commenced his apprenticeship at book and job printing, under the instruction of Jacob B. Moore, who carried on the business extensively in the Main Village of Concord, N. H.[1] Having continued with Mr. Moore until he was twenty-one

---

[1] Printing is one of the most extensive branches of business in Concord. The first newspaper printed there appeared January 6, 1790, and was called the "Concord Herald and New Hampshire Intelligencer." It was printed on a sheet fourteen by nine inches, and had for its motto: "The PRESS is the CRADLE of science, the NURSE of genius, and the SHIELD of liberty." In the course of time this paper was discontinued and succeeded by the "New Hampshire Patriot," "New Hampshire Statesman," "Congregational Journal," "Independent Democrat," "Democratic Standard," and several others. Mr. J. B. Moore, referred to in the text, had an extraordinary business talent. He was a master-printer, proof-reader, bookseller and publisher, editor of a newspaper, proprietor of a bookbindery, which was under his management, recorder of deeds, secretary of the New Hampshire Historical Society, &c. His father belonged to the medical profession; his two brothers, Henry and John, were printers and distinguished musicians.

years of age, Samuel soon afterward went to Boston, where he worked at printing a while. In short, he devoted ten years to travelling and printing before making a permanent abode. When he was in the western country, in 1828, his mother said to me one morning, " I shall never see our son Samuel again on earth, for in my sleep last night I heard his sighs and groans, and felt that this child, whom I have loved so well, will not come home while I am alive." She indeed died before his return. At the time she heard the groans in her sleep, he was dangerously sick in Bedford, Pa., but the circumstance of his sickness was unknown to her.

At the age of twenty-five years, he married a young lady in Philadelphia, whose father was a southern merchant. Soon after marriage he went with his wife to Cincinnati, where, before the expiration of a year from the time of their arrival in that city, she died.

During the time I have lived in West Concord, there have been erected on Long Pond BROOK below my saw-mill a number of buildings, and the following account relating to their uses, and other matters pertaining to the village, was written, in 1836, by Samuel, while on a visit to his old home here.

" CONCORD WEST PARISH VILLAGE contains eighteen dwelling-houses, and, beside other useful establishments, a store, tavern, shoemaker's, and carpenter's shop. It is situated on the western side of, and half a mile from, the Merrimac River, which sometimes overflows its fertile banks. A neat meeting-house with a bell (occupying ground once owned by my father, which he, my two brothers, and myself have tilled) gives to the village an air of some importance, and indicates a spirit of religious feeling among its inhabitants. The scenery of the village and surrounding country is interesting. Alas! where are the companions of my early days, — the boys and girls with whom I associated when a boy? Many of the people, old and young, whom I knew in former years, are dead! My MOTHER and sister Mary are not here, and no more will they behold the village. I saw my mother for the last time, soon after serving my apprenticeship, as she stood at a front window of our house, looking at me while I was getting into a sleigh with my father, who carried me to 'The Street,' whence I went the next day to Boston. As I rode from the house down the gentle slope, my eyes were turned toward my mother, who, still at the window, signified by moving her hand, *a farewell to me!* I remember many of her kind words of instruction. On taking up a volume of William Penn's Works, she said to me, 'Strive, my son, to be as good as the Friend who wrote this book.' . . .

"A brick dwelling-house occupies the site of the old *school-house*, where I ' Once learned to read

my A B C,' and where Peter C. Farnum did *not*
use his ferule upon my hands, but applied this cor-
recting instrument to the palms of *some* of his
scholars.[1] He was, most assuredly, 'a gentleman
and a scholar.' He taught one winter near the
south end of Long Pond. In going to and return-

[1] In " The Poetical Works of John Greenleaf Whittier,"
is a poem entitled, " To my old Schoolmaster : an Epistle not
after the manner of Horace," from which I extract the following : —

> " OLD friend, kind friend ! lightly down
> Drop time's snow-flakes on thy crown !
> Never be thy shadow less,
> Never fail thy cheerfulness.
> I, the urchin unto whom,
> In that smoked and dingy room,
> Where the district gave thee rule
> O'er its ragged winter school,
> Thou didst teach the mysteries
> Of those weary A B C's, —
>
> .   .   .   .
>
> I, — the man of middle years,
> In whose sable locks appears
> Many a warning fleck of gray, —
> Looking back to that far day,
> And thy primal lessons, feel
> Grateful smiles my lips unseal,
> As, remembering thee, I blend
> Olden teacher, present friend,
> Wise with antiquarian search,
> In the scrolls of state and church ;
> Named on history's title-page,
> Parish-clerk and justice sage ;
> For the ferule's wholesome awe
> Wielding now the sword of law."

ing from the school-house, when the surface of the Pond was frozen, he would skate across it. He is dead, but his widow, a good and pleasant woman, still lives. The 'Widow Farnum's' house is shaded by a large elm-tree. A little distance therefrom is an unpainted domicile, more than a century old, in which lives John Elliot. In front of it were formerly two great willow-trees. The trunks are still there. The little children of the village, as they see the aged Elliot walking along the road, are wont to say, 'There goes the old Revolutioner.' And that comical genius 'Judge' Reed, with a double chin, a soldier of the war of 1812–15, is — I know not where.

"But where is my little water-wheel and the apparatus attached to it in imitation of a saw-mill, that I, many years ago, caused to be worked by the water of the BROOK flowing from the great Pond? They have passed away! Well, my father's old saw-mill is still at work, and he saws laths and shingles in the lower part of the building. The water escapes, mingled with saw-dust, from his mill, and rapidly ripples along thirty-five rods, when it is obstructed by a dam and made to work machinery for sawing laths, shingles, wood for *matches*, and to grind tanners' bark, gypsum or Plaster of Paris, etc. 'Matches,' saith a poet, 'are made in Heaven;' but those called *Lucifer* are made in this village, and *girls* are employed in wrapping them in paper. A few steps below these works, the 'purling' BROOK is subjected to a dam for the benefit of a blacksmith's shop with a trip-hammer, and a lead-pipe manufactory. After leaving the great wheel of this shop, the water, formed into a pond on the west side of the main road, is conveyed by a sluice under it to a brick edifice on the opposite side. This building, used for a grist-mill, occupies the place where stood a wooden grist-mill which was erected fifty years ago, by Messrs. Howe and Duston.[1]

[1] During the last twenty-five years, West Concord Village has undergone many changes. The inhabitants who had grown old before that time have "gone to that bourne whence no traveller returns," and their places are now filled by some of their descendants, who occupy the old homesteads, surrounded by their children and grandchildren. The old wooden school-house has been demolished, and replaced by one of brick, which contains two large rooms on the first story, and a spacious hall on the second. The old tavern building is occupied as a boarding-house. One store, one carpenter's, one wheelwright's, one shoemaker's, two blacksmith's shops, a post-office, a station of the Concord and Claremont Railroad, &c., are in the village, which contains sixty families, with a population of nearly three hundred. The former little pond, which was situated a short distance below the old saw-mill, and whose waters gave motion to a bark-mill, etc., has been greatly enlarged by the Holdens, who have erected just below it a brick building 130 feet long and three stories high, called "The New Factory," in which are manufactured extra white flannels. The old brick edifice below, formerly used for a grist-mill, was built by Dr. Peter Renton and John Jarvis, at a cost of about twelve thousand dollars, and converted by the Holdens into a factory for the

" From the eastern side of the road to the ground below, the depth is twenty feet. When the old mill occupied the site of the new one, the side of the road on which the mill stood was not guarded by a railing. One day, when a lady was riding past in a chaise, the horse became frightened and began to back toward that side of the road. The lady,

manufacture of woollen blankets of an excellent quality. This mill was partially destroyed by fire, several months ago, but has been completely repaired with additions; both factories are warmed by steam, and the number of operatives in them is about eighty. The next mill below is called " The Mackerel Kit Factory," where twelve men are employed; they use five hundred cords of saplings in the manufacture of eighty thousand mackerel kits. The refuse wood readily sells at the factory for two dollars per cord; the trimmings and shavings also are sold there, and farmers buy the saw-dust for manure.

Concord comprises about 41,000 acres, of which 1000 are covered with the water of brooks, ponds, and rivers; the names of the ponds are LONG, Turkey, Turtle, Horse-shoe, Snow, and Hot-hole. The people of Concord have not neglected to avail themselves of the advantages derived from WATER-POWER.

" The lapse of time and rivers is the same;
  Both speed their journey with a restless stream.
  The silent pace with which they steal away,
  No wealth can bribe, nor prayers persuade to stay.
  Alike irrevocable both when past,
  And a wide ocean swallows both at last.
  Though each resemble each in ev'ry part,
  A diff'rence strikes at length the musing heart:
  Streams never flow in vain; where streams abound,
  How laughs the land with various plenty crowned!"

aware of her danger, succeeded in jumping from the chaise, but the horse and vehicle were precipitated to the ground below!

"The water, after leaving this mill, is soon dammed again, and made to work machinery for carding wool, dressing cloth, &c. Once more free it flows, — and

"'How without malice murmuring, glides its current!
O sweet simplicity of days gone by!'—

a meandering, rippling course through a low woodland and fertile interval fields till it mingles with the waters of the Merrimac. Now farewell, useful BROOK,

"'Laugh of the mountain!— lyre of bird and tree!
Pomp of the meadow! mirror of the morn!
The soul of April, unto whom are born
The rose and jessamine, leaps wild in thee!'"

In 1837 Samuel went to Cambridge, Mass., where he has since lived and pursued the printing business, and where, at different times, I have been to visit him. Here he married into a family concerning whom I have learned some particulars of interest, such as the following:—

Governor Hutchinson (who did *not*, according to John Adams, aid the people of Massachusetts in their struggles to get the *Tea* back to London) had a niece who was born Jan. 18, 1755, and died Oct. 20, 1851, aged 96 years, 9 months, and 2 days. She liked a good cup of *tea*, had a remarkable memory, and was fond of relating stories about what she saw and heard when young. She had two sisters and seven brothers. Her brothers were accustomed to *knit their own stockings*, and frequently sat together, so engaged, around their father's fire. Her maiden name was Hutchinson, and she married a Mr. Learned, one of their sons being named DAVID, who married ELIZA P. MARSH, a descendant of General Israel Putnam. During one of my visits at Cambridge, David's wife told me that once, while riding in a stage to Danvers, she pointed to a school-house and remarked to one of her daughters, who accompanied her, that she used to go to school there when a young girl. Whereupon an old gentleman, in the stage, said, —

"Did you? Well, so did I go to school there when a boy. The young lady, then, who sits by you, must be your daughter, for she looks like a girl by the name of Eliza Putnam Marsh, who went to school at the time I did. Was not that your name?"

Mrs. Learned replied in the affirmative. The aged gentleman then continued, saying, "Before you pointed out the school-house, I thought that you and the young lady, sitting by you, belonged to the Putnam race."

This incident caused some merriment in the stage. Mrs. Learned relates another anecdote: Her grandfather, Henry Putnam, while fighting at Lexington, on the 19th of April, 1775, was wounded by a bullet in his left arm, and his eldest son was killed in the same battle. Her grandfather was carried to his house in Danvers, where the bullet was extracted. While lying in his bed, on the 16th of June following, he said to his wife, who was thoughtfully walking about the room, " Why are you so serious ? " She in reply said, " Soon there will be another fight with the British soldiers." " Then," rejoined he, with much animation, " bring my gun to me that I may ascertain whether I can fire it." The gun, already loaded, was brought to him, and he soon discharged it through an open window. Early in the morning of the memorable SEVENTEENTH, Henry Putnam, although his arm was in a dangerous condition, persuaded his wife to take him in a chaise to the foot of Breed's Hill. He fought in the battle of " Bunker Hill," and was wounded in one of his legs. He lived to be quite old. His house is now standing in Danvers.

The before-mentioned David Learned[1] and his wife, Eliza P., had eight children,[2] two sons and six

---

[1] He died in Cambridge, May 8, 1838, aged 48 years.

[2] Named Lydia P., Henry, Laura, Olive, Elizabeth, Fanny, William, and Eliza Ann. Henry married Catharine Lopez, and several years afterward moved with his family to Kansas Territory, where he experienced his full share of troubles about slavery. In the spring of 1859 he went to Pike's Peak, with many friends, in search of gold. In 1861, with the same object in view, he travelled, accompanied by his son, who is now an officer in the Federal Army, through parts of New Mexico and Utah Territory, and beyond the San Juan Mountains. During this adventure they saw a boiling-hot spring, thirty feet in diameter and fathomless; they cooked meat in it. The hot water runs a short distance and empties

daughters. One of these, Lydia Putnam, who was born Dec. 7, 1817, my son Samuel married, in Cambridge, Feb. 25, 1841; their children were:—

1. Charles Gordon, born Jan. 9, 1842, died June 30, 1848, aged 6 years, 5 months, and 21 days; 2. Emma Louisa, born April 26, 1843; 3. Annie Eliza, born May 19, 1845; 4. George Cooledge,[1]

into the San Juan River. Henry's sister Elizabeth went to Lawrence City, Kansas Territory, in 1859, and, in the following year, was married to Mahlon K. Moore. Soon after marriage they moved to Colorado Territory, where she died March 13, 1862, aged 34 years. "I have sad news for you all!" wrote her brother Henry to his relatives in Massachusetts. "Our sister Lizzie is deceased! I am overwhelmed with grief at this unexpected event! Yet I derive consolation from the reflection that her spirit is in a happier world than this. . . . She was universally beloved by her many friends dwelling in this distant land. Her remains were carried to Denver, where they were buried. The funeral ceremonies were solemn and impressive, a large number of her friends being present on the occasion. . . . Mahlon is exceedingly afflicted by the loss of his dear wife." . . .

[1] He died in Cambridge, June 17, 1860, of phthisis, aged 12 years and 8 months. Until the last two months before his death, he had intermediate times of amusing himself in various ways. Reading was his great delight. He seemed from day to day to get wisdom and understanding. Sometimes he would say, "Oh! I wish I could feel well one whole day!" He did not like any allusion to death, but desired to get well that he might accomplish good works. Until almost the last moment of his life, he retained his mind in its full vigor. Just before he ceased to breathe, he repeatedly said, "Can't you see it? I can see it as plain as day." The pleasant, joyful manner in which he uttered these words, gave

born Oct. 17, 1847; 5. Louis Gordon, born July
25, 1850; 6. the sixth child, born July 20, 1849,
died in infancy.

The remains of Charles Gordon, the first of the
above-named children, were deposited in the rural
and delightful Mount Auburn Cemetery.[1] Shortly
after he died I received from his father a letter,
from which the following is an extract : —

. . . " I cannot write POETRY, but will try to
give you an idea of my wife's and of my own

assurance to those by his side that a vision of delight cheered
the last moments of his life on earth. The closing happy
scene of his terrestrial career, reminds one of the words of an
evening hymn : —

> " Teach me to live, that I may dread
> The grave as little as my bed ; " &c.

" 'T is held that sorrow makes us wise." And it is said
that " the death of children seems, *primâ facie*, unnatural.
In so far as the unnaturalness of death consists in taking the
living away in the progress of development and usefulness,
it pervades all ages."

> " I will not say God's ordinance
> Of Death is blown in every wind ;
> For that is not a common chance
> That takes away a noble mind.
>
> .   .   .   .   .
>
> " Sleep sweetly, tender heart, in peace ;
> Sleep, holy spirit, blessed soul,
> While the stars burn, the moons increase,
> And the great ages onward roll."

[1] His body was a few years afterward removed to the new
Cambridge Cemetery. The earthly remains of Charles and
George now lie side by side

feelings at the time and after our Charles Gordon died : —

" THE DEATH OF CHARLES GORDON HUTCHINS.

" ' O let the soul her slumbers break,
Let thought be quickened and awake;
Awake to see
How soon this life is past and gone,
And death comes softly stealing on,
How silently ! '

" Oh, CHARLES ! we hear no more thy voice, —
No more with thee do we rejoice !
Thy life was short, thy years were few, —
Six summers only didst thou view !
And yet how much in those few years —
Those years so full of hopes and fears —
We heard thee say, — we saw thee do,
To keep thy image in our view !

" We saw thee in thy happy play
Amuse thyself from day to day;
Thy joyous notes of song and glee
Imparted bliss to us and thee.
Thy plays did give thee great delight,
And oh ! it was a happy sight
To see thee, in thy youthful prime,
Enjoy the moments of thy time.

" Thy playthings we behold with tears,
For something whispers in our ears,
And seems all mournfully to say,
That ' Death has taken CHARLES away ! '
Oh, yes ! he 's dead ! — *we saw him die !*
We saw his fix'd — his sightless eye !
And yet, with true affection warm,
We gaz'd upon his lifeless form !

"It was in June, when birds do sing,
And make the air with music ring,
That CHARLIE saw no more the light,
And pass'd from ev'ry mortal's sight!
Ere winter's frost had disappear'd,
His countenance was often cheer'd
With pleasing thoughts of summer's charms, —
But ah! *he died in Death's cold arms!*"

While I was once at a Friends' Meeting, a Friend arose and gave utterance to these words: "THIS LIFE IS UNCERTAIN, BUT DEATH IS CERTAIN." To which may be appropriately added the following: The Lord "knoweth our frame; He remembereth that we are dust. As for man, his days are as grass; as a flower of the field he flourisheth. For the wind passeth over it and it is gone; and the place thereof shall know it no more."

CHAPTER IX.

AN ACCOUNT OF SOME BUSINESS IN WHICH I ENGAGED, EMBRACING A PARTICULAR NOTICE OF EMBARRASS-MENTS WHICH A CERTAIN MAN CAUSED ME. — CHEER-ING COUNSEL. — AGRICULTURAL PURSUITS. — AN INCI-DENT RESPECTING A CLOCK. — LAWYERS.

IT has been said that " wars[1] drive up riches in heaps, as winds drive up snows, making and concealing many abysses." During our last war with England, an enormous capital was invested in manufacturing establishments in the United States. While the war continued, our country was abund-antly supplied with articles from these establish-ments ; but after the peace, British goods were im-ported into the United States in such quantities, that our manufacturers suffered severe embarrassments ;

---

[1] The following lines relate to the deplorable civil war in our country : —

> " With one red flare, the lightning stretch'd its wing,
>   And a rolling echo rous'd a million men !
>   Then the ploughman left his field ;
>   The smith at his clanging forge,
>   Forged him a sword to wield ;
>   From meadow and mountain-gorge,
>   And the western plains they came,
>   Fronting the storm and flame."

indeed, many of them were broken down. I — one of the many persons who undertook to manufacture cotton cloth, at the time referred to — erected a large building immediately below my saw-mill, set up five hand-looms in one of its second-story rooms, and fitted up an adjoining room for clock-making. In the attic I had an apparatus for winding thread on bobbins, and the lower apartment of the building was used for storage. My looms were in operation three years. I purchased a considerable quantity of iron castings for machinery, as I intended to enlarge my factory operations, but power-looms came into general use, and I did not carry my intention into effect. In short, I sustained a considerable loss from an outlay for machinery, some of which I used for firewood, and the iron works I sold by auction at a nominal price.

Thus ended my weaving business, but I continued to make clocks for twenty years afterward. In 1818 John Slater, whose brother Samuel, in connection with a Mr. Brown, built the first cotton factory in the United States, in Rhode Island, came to my house with a view to purchase my mill privilege. After examining it he said to me, " I am disposed to make you a proposition, namely: if a number of citizens of Concord will become partners with me, and will invest one half of the capital necessary to build an extensive cotton factory on this mill privilege, I will invest the other half, and forthwith commence building the factory, provided you will sell us the mill privilege at a fair price." I replied satisfactorily to his proposition, and we exerted ourselves to induce Concord capitalists to engage in the enterprise, but they declined, and I retained possession of the mill privilege.[1]

That I might reduce the amount of my pecuniary

[1] The following items are selected from an article in the Writings of Levi Woodbury, LL. D., on the Cultivation, Manufacture, and Foreign Trade of Cotton : —

" In the 16th century, cotton manufactures came to Europe from India, through the trade of Venice; . . . they were introduced into China from India about 200 years earlier. . . . They existed in Arabia in the 7th century; found in America when discovered, at the close of the 15th century.

" 1730. First cotton yarn spun in England by machinery, by Mr. Wyatt.

" 1742. First mill for spinning cotton built at Birmingham; moved by mules or horses; but not successful.

" 1790. First cotton factory built in the United States, in Rhode Island. Water power first applied to the mule spinner, by Kelly.

" 1793. The cotton-gin invented by Eli Whitney, in the United States.

" 1803. First cotton factory built in New Hampshire.

" 1805. Power-looms successfully and widely introduced into England, after many failures.

. . . " The power-loom introduced into the United States first, at Waltham, Mass., in 1815.

" 1822. First cotton-factory erected at Lowell.

" In England three times as many spindles and factories are moved by steam as by water.

" The United States, by numerous and cheap waterfalls, have a good substitute for steam."

indebtedness to a number of persons, I sold three parcels of my land, for which I received an equivalent in money. I sold to Number One — I avoid giving the names of persons — another lot of good tillage land for a sum of money, not more than one fifth part of which did I receive, notwithstanding I took a mortgage on the land at the time of sale. Being indebted to that honorable and excellent man, Number Two, who held a mortgage on my property, I was requested by him to make a payment. As I could not, he borrowed money of Number Three, and passed the mortgage he held on my property into Three's hands, as security for the money loaned. Number Three then said to me, " I will give you a year in which to redeem this mortgage; if it is not redeemed in that time *I shall foreclose it!* "

I hired a sum of money of Number Four, and assigned him as a security in part for payment, the mortgage I held on the land that I sold to Number One. But the act of my application to him for money with which to clear myself of Number Three, was " like jumping out of the frying-pan into the fire! " Or in other words, in attempting to steer my business-ship clear of Scylla, I ran it against Charybdis. Number Four's loan of the sum of money to me is connected with the last named mortgage; but I will briefly say, that after he had possession of the mortgage a few days, Number Two and I rode to his house to obtain it for a particular purpose. Number Four's father had accumulated much property, on the principle, perhaps, of "get money, honestly if you can, but *get money!*" He was sitting by the side of his son, and, after listening to what I said, they withdrew to an adjoining room. On their return, Four's father said, "*We* have concluded *not* to let anything be done with the mortgage!"

This announcement fell like a thunderbolt upon me! I solicited them in vain to change their decision; and the reasoning of my learned friend, Number Two, was entirely disregarded by them. Number Four, regardless of justice toward me,

.   .   .   .

.   .   .   .

.   .   .   .

.   .   .   .   I can forgive but not forget these acts. A Christian says, that "a forgiveness ought to be like a cancelled note, torn in two and burned up, so that it never can be shown against the man."

Before I hired the money, I requested Number Four to send me several fleeces of wool, which I received, but they came mixed with extraneous matter, not ordered. I sustained a considerable loss in this trade with him; he tried also to injure me in the clock-making business. Remembrances of this kind are unpleasant. "If a man meets with injustice," says a preacher of the Gospel, "it is not required that he shall not be roused to meet it; but if he is angry after he has had time to think upon it, that is sinful; the flame is not wrong but the coals are." I have always made it my aim not to return evil for evil. I was unjustly treated by Number Four, but had no will to do him a wrong. I paid his demand against me, believing then as now that he acted wrongfully toward me. " If a man has done wrong, his own thoughts should turn him to reparation; but if they do not, the first intimation from the injured person should suffice." My intimation to Number Four did not cause him to make me any reparation or amends of any kind. He and his father have gone down to their graves, and the Almighty Ruler of the universe will justly reward them for their deeds on earth. They accumulated wealth, but " He that loveth silver shall not be satisfied with silver." They were religious men; but some men like religion "as a sort of lightning-rod to their houses, to ward off, by and by, the bolts of divine wrath."

I had met with pecuniary losses to a considerable amount, but the wise and cheering counsel of my wife, and the kindness and industry of our children, encouraged me to persevere in business. Idleness is not a part of my nature.[1] I have always been industriously engaged in employments, which I not only deemed respectable but beneficial. Al-

[1] " Few minds wear out; more rust out. Sad thoughts attend upon folded arms. It is action that doth keep the mind sweet and sound."

though Number Four had been the cause of depriving me of much valuable property in land, yet my farm still embraced twenty-five acres, which, with the saw-mill on my water privilege, and my clock-making business, gave me ample means for support. My agricultural pursuits were generally attended with good success. "Not that which men do worthily, but that which they do successfully, is what history makes haste to record." Persons, on visiting my garden while teeming with a variety of vegetable plants, have applauded its appearance. One year I received a premium from the Agricultural Society of New Hampshire for having one of the best gardens.

But two unfortunate circumstances in relation to onions and hops are worthy of record. One season I sowed an acre of good land with onion-seed, but the land, the seed, and my labor produced only a cart-load of worthless scallions!

When hops were in great demand, and selling for fifty cents a pound, I planted an acre and a half of land with the roots. I gathered an excellent crop of hops the second year of their growth. When dried and packed they weighed seven hundred pounds, but — the price of the article had fallen! Refusing the offer of twelve cents per pound for my hops, I shipped them to New York. They were spoiled by heat, and I did not receive a copper for the whole lot!

A clock that I sold to a man in Vermont, after

running well for more than a year, became disordered, and was returned to me to be put in repair, which was done, and I charged the man two dollars for my labor. This trifling sum he refused to pay; I retained the clock, and he brought an action against me for *trover;* the decision being awarded in his favor, I was required to pay $100. I offered to make payment in clocks, but with this proposition the man would not comply. The result was, that by going to jail in Hopkinton for thirty days, I easily cleared myself of paying the $100. Having the limits of the jail-yard, which embraced the whole village, I boarded with a respectable and intelligent family, and employed nine or ten hours each day in working upon two clocks that I had engaged to have ready for delivery at a specified time. The Vermont man gained nothing from his parsimony in withholding the two dollars which he justly owed me. It frequently happens that those who have the most money, derive the greatest benefit from a resort to pleadings or tergiversations in court. "When lawyers flourish, there is a certain sign that the laws do not; for this flourishing can only arise from the perplexity or violation of them. If an English lawyer is in danger of starving in a market-town or village, he invites another and both thrive."

CHAPTER X.

DEATH OF MY FATHER AND OF HIS WIFE LUCY. — MY
WIFE'S LAST ILLNESS AND DEATH. — MEASURES THAT I
ADOPTED RELATIVE TO MY PROPERTY. — AN INCIDENT
PERTAINING TO MY BROTHER EZRA. — HIS REMOVALS.
— HIS DEATH AND THAT OF HIS WIFE. — MY BROTHER
ABEL'S WIFE'S DEATH, SHORTLY FOLLOWED BY HIS. —
A FUNERAL DISCOURSE. — CONCLUSION.

OF my father I have yet to say a few words
more. Many of his grandchildren well remember him as he used to go about visiting his
relatives, bent by the cares and toils of life, but
cheerful and happy. He received several slight
wounds while fighting against his country's foes.
In old age he[1] occasionally exhibited his scars to
some of his grandchildren, telling them that he had
been in the wars. If sometimes they saw upon
him a patched garment, they greeted him none the
less kindly, although they may not have known,
that he had sacrificed much of his property to aid

---

[1] I remember when I was about six years old, that he was
at my father's house and passed one night there. He showed
me two scars, saying, " When you are a man you will not forget that I let you see these." A few weeks afterward, my
sister Ednah and I dined with him and his wife at his house.
They were very kind and pleasant toward us. He showed
me in his cellar, his great potato-bin, full of that esculent
vegetable.

his country in her struggle for liberty. He[1] died in his house in Concord, Dec. 8, 1815, aged 82

[1] COLONEL GORDON HUTCHINS was a man of action. The distinguishing trait of his character was activity. Idleness stood aloof from him. His birth, different places of residence, avocations, &c., may be summed up thus: He was born in 1733; lived in Harvard, Mass., some time before 1744, and for several years after; went on a military expedition, when quite young, up the Kennebec River to Canada; married Dolly Stone, prior to 1758, in Harvard, where he was Constable, in 1766, and pursued the occupation of farming, &c.; moved, in 1773, to Concord, N. H., where he commenced the business of merchant; raised, in the spring of 1775, a military Company, was elected Captain of the same, marched to Medford, fought in the battle of Bunker Hill, and in that of White Plains; was raised to the rank of Lieutenant-Colonel; chosen Representative to the Provincial Congress held at Exeter; took an active and beneficial part in measures relative to the battle of Bennington; lived again in Concord, in 1778, following the mercantile business, and lost a considerable amount of property by the depreciation of the currency; in the following year went on a nautical adventure, and married Lucy Lund; moved, in 1780, to Pembroke, where he carried on farming until April, 1783; then moved to Coventry, where he built a grist-mill, dwelt there about a year, and then moved to Haverhill, where he lived several years, pursuing the business of farming; moved, in 1793, or before, to Rumney, where again he followed the same business for a number of years, and finally went back to Concord, and there, in a good old age, he ended his earthly career in 1815. His life extended through a stirring and eventful time in the world's history, — a period in which Napoleon Bonaparte commenced his military career at Toulon, and ended it on the battle-field of Waterloo; and during which, the Irish Rebellion and the Union between Ireland and England

years.   The funeral ceremonies took place at my
brother Abel's house, where many relatives and
friends of the deceased assembled, who afterward
followed the body to the grave.   On entering the
old burial-ground, in Concord, where now repose
in silence the remains of many of the early settlers
here, one may see, after passing along the main
pathway a short distance, a marble monument
which marks the grave of

C_olonel_ GORDON HUTCHINS.

By the side of it may also be seen a time-worn
slate slab, which designates the place where repose
the remains of his first wife, D_olly_ H_utchins_.

L_ucy_, his second wife, departed this life Jan. 4,
1833, aged 76 years, 3 months, and 10 days, in
Merrimac, where her remains were buried.

We, who now live, are hastening onward to the

took place; the Stamp Act was passed; the American Revolutionary War, and the War of 1812–15 between Great
Britain and the United States, transpired.   He lived, indeed,
at a "time that tried men's SOULS," and he was able and
proud to show honorable scars, which should testify through
his life that, knowing his country's rights, he had dared to
defend them.   He had a high sense of truth, justice, and
honor.   "I condole with you," see page 52, "as I always took
you to be a gentleman of Honor and Probity."   And his advice to his son Levi was, "ALWAYS KEEP GOOD COMPANY."
Through life his conduct manifested that he put his trust in
God, and his gray hair did NOT go down in sorrow to the grave.

> "The grave 's the pulpit of departed man,
>   From it he speaks — his text and doctrine is —
>   T_hou_, TOO, MUST DIE!"

grave. They, I believe, performed life's duties well. It is said that "the proper office of religion is to allay our terror of death, by exciting hopes of happiness beyond it."

In 1826 my wife began to be afflicted with a cancer, and toward the close of the following year suffered severely from its effects. In the ensuing summer she was relieved for a while by a surgical operation, and enjoyed a visit from our daughter Ruth; but in the autumn of 1828 the disease recommenced with renewed virulence, and she died in the following spring, April 2, aged 62 years, 11 months, and 17 days. A few weeks before this event, a Unitarian clergyman came to my house and had an interview with her. Subsequently he told me that he never had received more beneficial instruction from any person.[1] "Her language," he

---

[1] This clergyman gave my father in writing the following, which was published in the Concord newspapers: —

"Being dead your departed wife yet speaketh. She speaketh to all who knew her in life, and witnessed her triumph at death. She was a kind and faithful parent, a virtuous and affectionate wife, an humble and devout Christian. Her examples were worthy of imitation by all, and the righteous would desire that their last end might be like hers. The closing scenes of her life bear witness that Christ was with her; that he had taken victory from the grave, the sting from death, and that he was her hope of glory. Suffering great pain under one of the severest maladies incident to humanity, she sustained herself through her Christian hopes, in perfect resignation, without impatience and without repining. No trace of fear, of doubt, or anxiety marked her countenance

remarked, "was sublime, and her pure Christian sentiments gave assurance that she had walked in the path that leads to eternal life."

My wife deceased forty years, one month, and nine days from the time we were married. During this time we lived together in harmonious union, she being my best earthly friend, and a true guide for our children to follow. "Blessed are the dead who die in the Lord." To her, death was a bright opening to a purer state of existence. It was no "dark entrance to a valley of shadow and gloom, through which the soul must walk fearfully and alone, but as the very gate of heaven, through which it passes to the glorious company of the redeemed." In the Friends' burial-ground, in Concord, now repose her[1] remains, near those of our deceased children, John and Mary.

Considering what I had learned by experience,

---

at the approach of death; and, at that solemn moment, she surrendered her spirit to God, who gave it, with the calmness with which an infant sleeps. She employed those seasons, in which she was relieved from suffering, in giving spiritual instruction to others, — exhorting them to that love to God and love to man, which should prepare them for happiness here and hereafter; she has now gone to reap the reward of her labors."

[1] "Died in this town, April 2, 1829, Phebe Hutchins, wife of Levi Hutchins, aged 63. She was for many years a worthy member of the Society of Friends, and manifested much of that spirit of universal love, which she believed ought to be felt and cherished for all." — *History of Concord*, by N. Bouton, D. D.

I resolved to be on my guard against the duplicity of men, and, being entirely clear of debt, divided my property among my children. They, except Anna who remained with me at home, were all settled in distant places. As I was entitled to a pension for my Revolutionary services, I caused my name to be entered, two years after my wife's death, on the pension-list. I should have made the application before her death, but waived it out of respect to her opinions.

In 1814 a military Company was organized in Concord, of such persons as were not enrolled in the militia. The Company was "to be in readiness, at a moment's warning, to act under the direction of the Commander-in-Chief, for the defence of the State." My brother Ezra became a member of this Company, and was chosen Ensign. In April, 1821, he moved to Andover, N. H., where he kept a tavern and cultivated a farm till November, 1824, when he removed to Bangor, Me., where he kept a hotel. He died in the city of Bangor, May 17, 1849, aged 78 years, 11 months, and 21 days; his wife died in that city, July 12, 1853, aged 84 years. They possessed happy dispositions, enjoyed much felicity in life, and verified the saying, that "Happiness and unhappiness are more qualities of mind than incidents of place or position." The remembrance of them is pleasing to me; many have been the times we have had social chitchats together at each other's houses.

My brother Abel's wife died March 28, 1853, aged 85 years, 5 months, and 26 days. On the 4th of April following he deceased, at the age of 90 years and 19 days. On the occasion of his burial,[1] the Phœnix Hotel was draped on the front with emblems of mourning, and a large assembly of people were present, together with the Masonic fraternity, who appeared in their regalia. He and I when young had become Freemasons;[2] soon after

[1] " Such is the course of nature, that whoever lives long must outlive those whom he loves and honors." My father being present at the time of this burial, and NINETY-TWO years old, may have thought, that " it is evident that the decays of age must terminate in death ; " but the time of his brother's decease appeared to him too soon. " There is no man," says Tully, " who does not believe that he may yet live another year ; and there is none who does not, upon the same principle, hope another year for his parent or his friend." " Mr. Abel Hutchins," I use the words of Rev. Dr. Bouton, " was a large, portly man, about six feet in height, of fair complexion, a little florid, blue eyes, and, on account of being near-sighted, always wore spectacles."

[2] In 1816 an oration, on freemasonry, was delivered before a large audience, including my father, his brother Abel, and myself, assembled in the old North Church. While the orator was eloquently portraying the advantages derived from being a brother mason, I noticed that tears in quick succession rolled down my uncle Abel's cheeks. Although my father manifested no very apparent " sign " of a " melting heart and brimful eye," yet he appeared much interested in all the speaker said. Many " brothers of the mystic tie " have read with emotion Robert Burns' " Farewell to the Brethren of St. James' Lodge, Torbolton," commencing with the following stanza : —

joining the Society of Friends I withdrew from the order, but he continued a member of it through life. His funeral sermon was preached by his pastor, in Concord, in the meeting-house of the Unitarian Congregational Society, from this text: "THOU SHALT COME TO THY GRAVE IN A FULL AGE, LIKE AS A SHOCK OF CORN COMETH IN HIS SEASON." "The centre of kindred," said the pastor, "is removed to the other world, that it may draw the affections up thither and make them purer and stronger, — to the other world, where Old Age and youth are alike unknown terms. . . . The old man and the aged woman,[1] having filled out the measure

> "Adieu! a heart-warm, fond adieu!
>   Dear brothers of the mystic tie!
> Ye favored, ye enlightened few,
>   Companions of my social joy.
> Though I to foreign lands must hie,
>   Pursuing Fortune's slidd'ry ba',
> Wi' melting heart, and brimful eye,
>   I 'll mind you still, though far awa'."

[1] When I last saw them at their house on State Street, I said, "How happy I am to see you look so remarkably well in your old age. The remembrance of two little incidents is vivid to me: one, aunt, is, that in the winter of 1817, I called at your house with my father's horse and sleigh, and took you with me to make a short visit at my aunt Matilda Wiggin's house in 'The Street.' The other incident, uncle, relates to you. Some time after the house, that you and my father once owned and occupied together, was destroyed by fire, I saw you in company with Messrs. Bradley, Walker, and Ayer. You were discussing subjects of importance relating to town affairs. At length you exhibited to

of their days, and borne life's burdens, and discharged life's duties well, have passed away to their rest and reward."

Yes, they have passed away; but it is consoling to believe that they exist in a better world. I have enjoyed much happiness in their society on earth; now I am happy in the thought, that, in due time, I shall be with them [1] in heaven.

them a drawing on paper, saying, ' How do you like this plan of the Hotel I am going to build on the site of the old house ? ' After examining it they expressed great approbation, and Mr. Ayer said, ' The building will be an ornament to Concord.'"

[1] Their son Hamilton, see pp. 64, 65, and William Ladd, see note 1, p. 60, were early associates of mine. William's mother once said to him and me, " Now, little boys, I hope you will have a good time while playing together to-day."

The following, pertaining to the Ladd family, are additions to note 2, page 61: Edward Luff and his wife's children were: 1. Edward Jackson, born April 4, 1843, died July 26, 1844; 2. Nathaniel Ladd, born Oct. 29, 1848; 3. Thomas, born Nov. 7, 1853. David Patterson and his wife's son, George Hasty, born Dec. 9, 1855, died July, 1856. A. A. Hall and his wife's children were: 1. Amy Johnson, born May 8, 1847; 2. Anna Morrow, born Nov. 3, 1848; 3. Eleanor Ladd, born Sept. 9, 1850; 4. Andrew Austin, born Dec. 9, 1852; 5. Azariah Theodore, born Aug. 1, 1855, died Sept. 19, 1857; 6. Mary Kate, born Dec. 20, 1859; 7. Nathaniel Dudley, born Dec. 24, 1862; 8. Josephine Elizabeth, born June 3, 1864. William Dudley and his wife's children were: 1. Georgiana Mary, born May 19, 1849; 2. Fred. Newton, born Jan. 21, 1859. William Corwin and his wife's children were: 1. Alfred Treadwell, born Sept. 4, 1856, died Jan. 4, 1857; 2. George Ladd, born Sept. 25, 1859; 3. William L., born Feb. 1, 1860; 4. Nathaniel Dudley, born Dec. 1, 1863. In the

In a preceding page [115] I made mention of Elizabeth Yeats, who was one of my family for several years.   It is with a high appreciation of her merits that I allude to her again.   She has arrived at a good old age.   At an early period of her life she joined the Society of Friends, and still holds fast to their doctrines.   " Her ways are ways of pleasantness, and all her [1] paths are peace."

I have enjoyed much happiness in visiting and receiving visits from my children.   My grandchildren [2] and great-grandchildren have imparted to me

last two lines of the above-mentioned note, Charles should be placed before " George," and Hutchins, after " Julia."

[1] She is now passing the evening of her days, in great tranquillity, with my sister Ruth's children, who are as much attached to her as if she were of kindred blood.

[2] The following poem, written by Rev. F. E. Abbot, of Beverly, Mass., relates to my son George C.   See p. 144, three bottom lines : —

" LAST WORDS OF A DYING CHILD.

" The little life is ebbing fast ;
How swift the moments flee !
Each look and gesture of the past
How plainly I can see !

" He starts, and, gazing in the air,
Exclaims in tones of glee,
Pointing to some sweet vision there, —
' O Mother ! *don't* you *see ?* '

" He lies upon the little bed,
And smiles with love on me ;
There shines a light about his head
That even I can see.

additional happiness. The troubles I have encountered were the result of circumstances connected with business, but all kinds of "troubles are often the tools by which God fashions us for better things." It is a joy to feel that there is a realm where shall be fully realized our aspirations after happiness. All human beings are God's children, and while upon earth they are in school. "No one cries when children, long absent from their parents, go home. Vacation morning is a jubilee." But death is the vacation morning of the pure in heart. I have been blessed with a long life, have enjoyed many good things of this world, and now feel prepared to enter the world to come.

> "But ere my quivering lips can say
>   The words that rush to me,
> My morning star is lost in day,
>   And I — *I* cannot see!
>
> "I strive in vain to pierce the gloom,
>   And catch heaven's brilliancy;
> My child has vanish'd in the tomb;
>   Alas! *I* cannot see.
>
> "Yet in thy mother's heart, my boy,
>   Which yearns and bleeds for thee,
> Are echoing still those words of joy, —
>   ' O Mother! *don't* you *see?*'
>
> "I'll trust in One who ever hears, —
>   'T is darksome night with me,
> My eyes are blind with scalding tears;
>   But, darling, *I shall see!*"

ADDENDA.

LOOKING back through the mists of time, I recall to memory many incidents relating to my father, and although some are trifling, yet a record of them here may not be out of place. A poet says, —

> "O Memory, wafted by thy gentle gale,
> Oft up the stream of Time I turn my sail."

Wafted by the gale of memory back to the days of my boyhood, I am reminded that my father then gave me, while we were walking together hand in hand up the road toward our house, thirty-five cents in small change, saying, "Samuel, thou art a little boy, but I am fifty years old, and have helped thee in thy young days. Now, as we grow older, wilt thou not help me?" "I truly will," was my reply. At another time he said to me, "I will take my powder-horn, &c., and go a-gunning; thou mayst go with me." As we were returning home, I said, "It is going to rain." "Then," rejoined he, "we 'll do as they do in Spain,—let it rain." Two years after these little incidents occurred, he had an extraordinary crop of clover hay; while carting it into his barn he laughingly said to one of his hired men, "My father used to say, 'I would as lief have a barn full of northwest wind as of clover hay.'"

One of my father's maxims was, "Early to bed and early to rise." Long before sunrise, in summer, he was accustomed to be at work in one of his fields; few men could *keep up* with him in using the hoe, and his work was not only quickly but well done. In winter he arose at four o'clock, and, after making a fire, would sit by the side of it a while; then feed his cattle, make a fire in his shop, and work there before breakfast. The last time in the evening that he attended to his animals in the barn, was at eight o'clock; for several years during boyhood, I made it a point to go with him on this errand, holding the lantern as an excuse for accompanying him, as in reality I did not like to have him go alone, fearing some accident might befall him. At this period of life, I often went with him when he rode in his wagon from place to place to sell cotton cloth and BRASS clocks; *wooden* timekeepers he would never make nor repair. During one of these journeys we stopped a while at Hanover, N. H., were he sold to a storekeeper a number of rolls of cloth, and then put in order a clock in a large dwelling-house opposite the store. The lady of the house asked him to sell her *five* yards of cotton cloth. "O no," replied he, smiling, "I am not a dealer in the article on so small a scale." "Then," rejoined she, "will you sell me a whole roll?" "Yes, yes," was the quick reply.

Of Daniel and Ezekiel Webster I have heard him relate the following anecdote: "One morning, while I was eating breakfast at the tavern kept by Daniel Webster's father, Daniel and his brother Ezekiel, little boys with dirty faces and snarly hair, came to the table and asked me for bread and butter. I complied with their request, not thinking that they would become, in the course of time, two very distinguished men. Daniel dropped his piece of buttered bread on the sandy floor, and the buttered side was *down*. On picking it up he showed it to me, saying, 'What a pity! Please to give me another piece of bread buttered on both sides, then if I let it fall *one* of the buttered sides will be up.'"

Of DANIEL WEBSTER, who was "cradled 'mid the granite hills" of New Hampshire, a poet says:—

"And now from height to height he strides amain,
    While luminous with truth his pathway glows;
Where others toil and strive to climb in vain
    He stands in calm, magnificent repose.

.   .   .   .   .

"He spake, and listening senates learn'd the law,
    Tracing each streamlet to its fountain source;

The nations heard his words with wondering awe
Reverberate till their rocky shores were hoarse.

   .   .   .   .   .

" But he has vanish'd from the walks of men,
  And we shall hear his thrilling voice no more;
Nor shall we e'er ' behold his like again,'
  Nor list from other lips such lofty lore."

My father had a large assortment of carpenters' tools, and used them in making various things. With but little assistance he built for himself a large barn. He made the looms for his factory and others which he sold. On his return from a visit to the Shaker village in Canterbury, N. H., he said, " I have seen a wonderful invention, — a machine for planting onion, beet, and carrot seeds," and forthwith made one for himself.

I once heard him relate to a friend, that he had in many instances exonerated his debtors, who were in indigent or unfortunate circumstances, from paying him. A farmer bought of him on credit a loom, used it a year, and then solicited him to take it back, which he did and required no pay for its use. Full often men, regardless of just principles in trade, selfish and grasping, " spend their lives in heaping up colossal piles of treasure, which stand, at the end, like the pyramids in the desert sands, holding only the *dust* of kings." But my father, governed by the principle, that " in all things what-soever ye would that men should do to you, do ye even so to them," manifested no disposition to ruin others in order to enrich himself.

As " a life of ease is not for any man, nor for any god," my father was not exempted from troubles. If, then, " the changes, which break up at short intervals the prosperity of men, are advertisements of a nature whose law is growth ; " if " with the wind of tribulation God separates in the floor of the soul the Chaff from the Corn ; " and if " the bad fortune of the good turns their faces up to heaven, and the good fortune of the bad bows their heads down to the earth," why should not men view their *calamities as blessings in disguise ?* [1]

---

[1] The following paragraphs, which I transcribe from a little book, entitled " Hebrew Tales," my father read with great interest : —

" Compelled by violent persecution to quit his native land, Rabbi Akiba wandered over barren wastes and dreary deserts. His whole equipage consisted of a LAMP, which he used to light at night, in order to study the Law, a COCK, which served him instead of a watch, to announce to him the rising dawn, and an ASS on which he rode.

" The sun was gradually sinking beneath the horizon, night was fast approaching, and the poor wanderer knew not where to shelter his head, or where to rest his weary limbs. Fatigued, and almost exhausted, he came at last near a village. He was glad to find it inhabited, thinking where human beings dwelt, there dwelt also humanity and compassion ; but he was mistaken. Not one of the inhospitable inhabitants would accommodate him. He was therefore obliged to seek shelter in a neighboring wood. ' It is hard, very hard,' said he, ' not to find a hospitable roof to protect me against the inclemency of the weather. But God is just, and whatever he does is for the best.'

" He seated himself beneath a tree, lighted his lamp, and

The trouble that " Number Four " caused my
father, had, at different times, the effect to depress

began to read the Law. He had scarcely read a chapter,
when a violent storm extinguished the light. 'What!' exclaimed he, 'must I not be permitted even to pursue my
favorite study? But God is just, and whatever he does is for
the best.'

" He stretched himself on the earth, willing, if possible, to
have a few hours' sleep. He had hardly closed his eyes, when
a fierce wolf came and killed the cock. 'What new misfor-
tune is this?' ejaculated the astonished Akiba. 'My vigilant
companion is gone! Who, then, will henceforth awaken me
to the study of the Law? But God is just; he knows what is
best for us poor mortals.'

" Scarcely had he finished the sentence, when a terrible lion
came and devoured the ass. 'What is to be done now?' exclaimed the lonely wanderer. 'My lamp and both of my
companions are gone, — all is gone! But praised be the
Lord, whatever he does is for the best.'

" He passed a sleepless night, and early in the morning
went to the village, to see whether he could procure a horse,
or any other beast of burden, to enable him to pursue his
journey. But what was his surprise, not to find a single in-
dividual alive! It appears that a band of robbers had entered the village during the night, killed its inhabitants, and
plundered their houses.

" As soon as Akiba had sufficiently recovered from the
amazement into which the wonderful occurrence had thrown
him, he lifted up his voice, and exclaimed, 'Thou great God,
the God of Abraham, Isaac, and Jacob, now I know by experience that poor mortal men are short-sighted and blind; often
considering as evils what are intended for their preservation!
But thou alone art just, and kind, and merciful! Had not
the hard-hearted people driven me, by their inhospitality, from
the village, I should assuredly have shared their fate. Had

his spirits. During one of these times my mother
said to him, " Do not be discouraged ; the Lord
will provide all things best for us. 'The Lord,'
says Solomon, is far from the wicked, but he heareth
the prayer of the righteous.' If in the Lord thou
putst thy trust He will bless thee and bring shame
upon those who do thee wrong." To which my
father pleasantly, but with an expression of deep
despondency, replied, " All I desire is death ! Give
me a little spot of ground — that is all ! "

Three or four months after this incident, while
my father was away from home on business, " Number Four" came to our house ; my mother, in the
course of conversation with him, made the inquiry,
" Canst thou not give my husband more time in
which to pay thy demand ? " He replied, " No ! "
My father, on returning home, heard the result of
" Four's" visit with sorrow. I said to him, " Why
are you so sorrowful ? " He replied, " Thou art
too young to understand the trouble that ' Number
Four' gives me." On one occasion he said to a
friend, " I am not rich, but perhaps I might have
been if I had done, in trade, by mankind as certain
persons have done by me."

He had a very good share of business prosperity,

not the wind extinguished my lamp, the robbers would have
been drawn to the spot and have murdered me. I perceive,
also, that it was thy mercy which deprived me of my two
companions, that they might not by their noise give notice to
the banditti where I was. Praised, then, be thy name forever
and ever ! "

enough for encouragement, and a sufficiency of adversity to check pride. "When flowers are full of heaven-descended dews, they always hang their heads; but some men hold theirs the higher the more they receive, getting proud as they get full." He possessed a well-balanced mind, and if he had met with no reverses in business, but had accumulated large possessions of wealth, he would not have held his head so high as to make it a target for envy to shoot at. He well knew that if those who are puffed up by the possession of riches, fail and go down, a multitude of people rejoice in their fall.

In 1844 my wife with our son, Charles Gordon, accompanied him in a journey from Cambridge, Mass., to Concord, N. H. They passed through Harvard, but made no stop there except that my father checked his horse to gaze on scenes of his childhood; for it is indeed true, as some sages have taught, that "man's good angel hovers over the place of his birth, and dwells with peculiar fondness on the days of his innocent childhood." Pointing to an old house, he said to Charles, "Look at that house; I was born in it, and I used to play on the ground in front when I was a little boy. On that ground my brother Abel and I wrestled together after eating a hearty supper of poached eggs, seventy years ago." This old dwelling-house is still standing, in 1864, and has been for a long time occupied by Nathan Willard, Sen. While riding through Harvard, with my wife and son, my father related to them other incidents of his early years, pertaining to hills, fields, etc., and doubtless some of his feelings are expressed in the following stanza : —

> " Ah, happy hills ! ah, pleasing shade !
>   Ah, fields beloved in vain !
> Where once my careless childhood strayed,
>   A stranger yet to pain !
> I feel the gales that from ye blow
> A momentary bliss below,
>   As waving fresh their gladsome wing,
> My weary soul they seem to soothe,
> And, redolent of joy and youth,
>   To breathe a second spring."

It is possible that, in reviewing on this occasion scenes of his youth, he inly said, " Many a boy I knew is dead, and many a girl grown old." Moreover, some of his thoughts and queries may, perchance, be expressed in the passage following : —

" The good old dames, in their white hoods and black-velvet gowns — their daughters, 'the cynosure of neighboring eyes,' — where are they all now, who, when they entered the church, used to divide men's thoughts between them and Heaven ? "

In 1850 he carefully examined all his accountbooks to correct errors he might find in them, and to learn the true condition of his business affairs. While so engaged he discovered, to his great surprise, that he was indebted to the amount of $38 to his old instructor in clock-making, Simon Willard, both parties having entertained the belief that their accounts were balanced. But when my father ascertained the case to be otherwise, two years after the death of Mr. Willard, he went to Roxbury and there found a daughter of Mr. Willard in needy circumstances. He gave her the $38, which she thankfully received, and shortly afterward invested in the purchase of a cow, that became a source of comfort and support to her as well as a memento, though a perishable one, of an honorable act. A few years before Mr. Willard's death, he came to Cambridge and put in order the tower-clock of the Unitarian church. As he passed through Harvard Square, a young lady, recognizing him, said to her companion, " That venerable man with silvery locks must be a good clock-maker, for he has grown gray in the occupation. He is what I should call a good *time-keeper* himself, for he has lived to enjoy a great deal of time."

My father's act when ninety years old, of causing a new dam to be built at Forge Pond, was very pleasing to him. " I often go up to my new dam," he wrote me, " but more frequently view it from the back-door of my house." From this door-way I have often seen him at work in his saw-mill, or in his shop; and I saw the BROOK and the HILL — well known by the sobriquet of Rattlesnake.

" The hills are dearest which our childish feet
    Have climbed the earliest; and the streams most sweet
   Are ever those at which our young lips drank,
    Stooped to their waters o'er the grassy bank ! "

My father gave to each of his six daughters and three sons a time-keeper. To me he gave one of these which he made soon after establishing the business of clock-making in Concord. It has no bell. "We take no note of time but from its loss; to give it then a *tongue* is wise in man."

As he was a musician in his youthful years, doubtless he did not forget, as he advanced in age, the tunes then familiar to him. While he was making clocks, I have often heard him — almost whistle. He became the owner of a musical clock which was much out of order. He put it into complete repair, and gave it to my brother John; it played seven different tunes.

After establishing himself as a clock-maker in "The Street," he frequently had occasion to travel to different parts of New England, on business, and as he grew older his fondness for travel increased; it did not forsake him in old age; consequently he went on a journey, three or four times a year, to transact some business or to visit his friends. When he was ninety years old, I heard him say, "As I travel from place to place I meet with old acquaintances who manifest toward me much kindness; and from many strangers I have received friendly regard. With many men I have had a pleasant intercourse through a period of forty years, without discovering in them a disposition to deceive or do otherwise than treat me well. In their society I have enjoyed real happiness, and their remembrance

12

is cheering to my old age." His visits at my house in Cambridge have imparted to my family and myself much happiness. On these occasions, having tarried with us a day or two, he would sometimes say, " I must go home, for if I do not Anna will think I am lost." To amuse him I frequently told him anecdotes, riddles, &c., among which was the following connumdrum, written by George Canning, Prime Minister to George II. : —

" There is a *word* of plural number,
A foe to peace and human slumber ;
Now any word you chance to take,
By adding *s* you plural make ;
But if an *s* you add to this,
How strange the metamorphosis !
Plural is plural then no more,
And sweet what bitter was before."

In vain he tried to think of the right word. " You know," said I, " that *cares* are bitter ; add an *s* to the word and you metamorphose it into *caress*, which is very sweet." During the last twenty years of his life my father read many books, among which were the works of Benjamin Franklin, John Adams, and Daniel Webster, the Madison Papers, the Orations and Speeches of Edward Everett, and Sparks' Life of Washington. On the margins of the pages of the last-named book, are many of his pencil-marks indicative of his admiration of Washington's character.

Having been an eye-witness of some of the scenes of the Revolutionary contest, he particularly noticed the following passages while reading some of Hon. Edward Everett's speeches : —

"I gaze with respectful admiration on these venerable men, the survivors, the few and sole survivors, of the eventful days in which they bore so honorable a part. One of them, Mr. Jonathan Harrington, who has this moment been assisted from the platform, ' FILLED THE FIFE ' on that morning of peril and glory at Lexington. . . . While I was helping that infirm old man, a few minutes since, to draw on his outer garment, as I saw him trembling with years, — the arm which held the FIFE on the nineteenth of April, 1775, now so feeble and nerveless, — I was ready to exclaim, since we have been alluding to him by the Christian name, 'I am distressed for thee, my brother Jonathan; very pleasant hast thou been unto me.' "

"The next letter is a treasure, for its author's sake. It was written by PUTNAM, on the immortal seventeenth; but written at Cambridge and before he went down to the battle. Here is the veteran's signature, of which I will only say it is somewhat doubtful whether it was made with a goosequill, the point of a cutlass, or the handle of a pickaxe. It announces the arrival of eighteen barrels of powder from Connecticut."

"When a war of self-defence, a war for those rights which make it life to live, is forced upon a people, it must be manfully met! That our Revolutionary contest was such a war, is now admitted by the consent of mankind."

In a letter that John Adams wrote in 1820 are these words: "I have great reason to rejoice in the happiness of my country, which has fully equalled, though not exceeded, the sanguine anticipations of my youth. God prosper long our glorious country, and make it a pattern to the world."

The fact that my grandfather fought in the battle of Bunker Hill, and that my father "filled the fife" a while in the struggle for American Independence, has been cherished in my remembrance with feelings of much pleasure, not unmixed with pride.

Mr. George W. Chase, author of the "History of Haverhill," says that the tune of the Americans at Bunker Hill was "Yankee Doodle."[1] It was

---

[1] The following version gives it as sung at least seventy years ago: —

"Father and I went down to Camp,
    Along with Captain Goodwin,
Where we *see* the men and boys
    As thick as hasty-*puddin*.

There was *Captain* Washington,
    Upon a slapping stallion,
A giving orders to his men —
    I *guess* there was a million.

"And then the feathers on his hat,
    They looked so *tarnal fina*,
I wanted *pockily* to get
    To give to my Jemima.

"And there they had a *swampin* gun,
    As large as log of maple,
On a *deuced* little cart —
    A load for father's cattle.

the first time of its use by them, but ever after it was their favorite, and has become our most popular national air. The story runs, that the song was composed by a British officer of the Revolution,

> " And every time they fired it off,
>   It took a horn of powder ;
>   It made a noise like father's gun,
>   Only a *nation* louder.
>
> " I went as near to it myself
>   As Jacob's *underpinnin,*
>   And father went *as near agin* —
>   I thought the *deuce* was in him.
>
> " And there I *see* a little *keg,*
>   Its heads were made of leather —
>   They knocked upon 't with little sticks
>   To call the folks together.
>
> " And there they 'd *fife away like fun,*
>   And play on *cornstalk* fiddles,
>   And some had *ribbons* red as blood,
>   All wound about their middles.
>
> " The troopers too would gallop up
>   And fire right in our faces ;
>   They *scared* me almost half to death
>   To see them run such races.
>
> " Old *uncle Sam* come there to change
>   Some pancakes and some onions,
>   For 'lasses-cakes, to carry home
>   To give his wife and young ones.
>
> " But I can't tell you half I *see,*
>   They kept up such a smother ;
>   So I took my hat off — made a bow,
>   And *scampered* home to — mother ! "

12 *

with a view to ridicule the Americans, who, by way of derision, were styled *Yankees*.

There is a time for all things, and consequently a time for rejoicing. When my father heard the news of peace, in 1815, between Great Britain and the United States, he was sitting in one of the front rooms of his house, holding a pair of tongs, which he instantly clapped together, expressing much joy.

In June, 1854, I commenced sending him a letter every week. The last time that he was at my house, he asked me, just before leaving, whether I had a letter ready for him to take home and read? On receiving a negative reply, he said, " Then I am sorry." He wrote his last letter to me in 1854, when he was ninety-two years and six months old. " I have thought," said he, " of leaving something [a sketch of his life], so that when I am gone and never more to return, you and others may look upon it and be reminded that such a being as Levi Hutchins once existed on the earth, and lived 76 years out of more than 92 without a single day of sickness." This letter, — see page 42, — contained these words: " I wish you to remember that in

1778 I was placed at Andover

His granddaughter, Mrs. Metford, passed several months at his house, in 1854–5, and while there wrote me a number of letters, the following being an extract from one of them : —

" In the evening grandpa read thy letter through and was highly entertained with its contents: indeed, he was exceedingly diverted with thy amusing account of Thanksgiving performances, in which thou, thy family, and other relatives took parts. He has not often made an effort at reading by lamplight, since I came here. Unless the sun is shining, he cannot see well to read anything. Fénélon and à Kempis, the print of which is large and clear, he often reads. His health is good and mind sound."

From another of her letters, dated at West Concord, June 6, 1855, I copy as follows: —

" Occasionally grandpa coughs, and, although he lies a greater part of the time upon his bed, yet he appears to have no disease. The circumstance of his lying a-bed in the daytime is so uncommon, that he smilingly remarked, ' Now I believe that Death is about to remove me to the delightful realms above.' His mental powers never were clearer; he is cheerful and happy, has given particular directions respecting his funeral, desires me and others to tell everybody how comfortably sick he is, and that he is favored now by his heavenly Father and always has been. And who can doubt this? No one ever saw a more striking example of a quiet; transplanting from the earthly to the heavenly home. There is no pleasanter or more exalting scene than to behold an aged man, in the full possession of intellect, gradually and happily passing heavenward. He is constantly attended by a number of his children and grandchildren, who strive to render him acts of kindness, for which he often expresses much gratitude."

On the 8th of June, 1855, with a little assistance, he arose from the bed, — a clock of his own manufacture meanwhile ticking away the seconds of time in a corner of the room, — put on his clothes, sat down by a window, drank a little coffee, and wound up his watch. As I witnessed this scene, and looked from the windows at the mill near by, or down the street and toward the river, or at the old orchard land: — as I beheld these things, in a moment, —

> " In that MOMENT o'er my soul
> Years of memory seem'd to roll."

After a while he lay down and conversed very cheerfully about his garden and various other matters. He continued to enjoy the full possession of his faculties, the company of attending relatives, and freedom from bodily or mental pains, until " the *wheels* of his time ceased to revolve, because their *pivots* had become so worn in their *sockets*, and their periphery so smooth, that no farther *repairing* could make them act reciprocally upon each other or for a longer time keep up the *motions* of life." Thus he quietly and happily departed from this world, on the 13th day of June, 1855, aged 93 years, 9 months, and 26 days. It has been truthfully remarked, that years and generations cease not to roll. The youngest, if they live, *must* be old, and the oldest *must* die. " There is a ripeness of time for death," said Thomas Jefferson, " regarding others as well as ourselves, when it is reasonable we should drop off, and make room for another growth. When we have lived our generation out, we should not wish to encroach on another. I enjoy good health. I am happy in what is around me ; yet I assure you, I am ripe for leaving all, this year, this day, this hour."

An author says, " Youth is the season of receptivity ; old age is for revision. Extreme age involves loss of power to act, but not so much loss of wisdom to judge. Old men, therefore, though less fitted for executive stations, are still the best of counsellors. Men, like growing fruit, should mellow as time advances ; but more frequently estranged from what is proper to them, like fruits prematurely gathered, they only decay into a semblance of ripeness. The finest of all accomplishments is that of growing old gracefully. Next to this is the merit of accepting the fact of old age with serenity and unfaltering courage. Among the most agreeable of companionships is that of an old man who has the art of making his company acceptable to the young. No man is entitled to be spoken of as an old man till he has turned seventy. Only at this period — a period still consistent with unimpaired intellectual vigor — does the reverence proper to age begin. And this view accords with that of the wise Frenchman, M. Flourens. ' The first ten years of life,' he says, 'are infancy, properly so called; the second ten is the period of boyhood; from twenty to thirty is the first youth; from thirty to forty, the second. The first manhood is from forty to fifty-five; the second from fifty-five to seventy. This period of manhood is the age of strength, the MANLY period of human life. From seventy to eighty-five is the first period of old age, and at eighty-five the second old age begins.'"

My father's remains were interred in the Friends' burial-ground, in Concord. Some months subsequent to his decease, one of his grandchildren said of him: "Grandpa's memory will ever be fondly cherished in the hearts of those who loved his pleasant ways, affectionate greetings, and agreeable company."

His person was well proportioned; stature nearly six feet; features regular and symmetrical;[1] eyes blue, and the expression of his countenance indicated thoughtfulness, and a good disposition. His manners were pleasant, courteous, and cheerful, and no one could justly entertain ill feelings toward him. He was candid and sincere; FRIENDS true and many he had, and he highly appreciated the kindnesses of all persons toward him. He was not actuated by sinister motives, and did not resort to unworthy means for the attainment of an end. Truth and justice found an abiding-place in his mind, and the

---

[1] "Thy father," said an aged lady to me, "was the handsomest man, in his youth, that I ever saw."

want of these virtues in those whom he had trusted, utterly destroyed his confidence in them. He believed that " man wants a religion to sustain his heart and afford it a rest which he cannot find within himself." His religious views were decidedly in accordance with those entertained by Friends ; for certain reasons, however, he withdrew from that Society several years before his decease. But to his last hours he was a true Friend in heart and principle. He was fond of reading the works of distinguished Friends, — of William Penn, Robert Barclay, and others. A framed likeness of William Penn he kept suspended under a looking-glass in the room where he passed much of his [1] time.

" The Quaker character," says Charles Lamb, " was hardened in the fires of persecution in the seventeenth century; not quite to the stake and fagot, but little short of that. They grew up and thrived against noisome prisons, cruel beatings, whippings, stockings. They have since endured a century or two of scoffs, contempts ; they have been a by-word and a nay-word ; they have stood unmoved ; and the consequence of long conscientious resistance on one part is invariably, in the end, remission on the other."

In business my father's desire was, that whatever work passed from his hands should be WELL done ; had he thought less of integrity and honor, and

[1] I once heard him say, " George Fox pointed out a rough path for mankind to walk in, but William Penn beautified it."

more of riches, he might have left more treasures
in gold, but less affection for him in the hearts of
his surviving friends.   *Deus eum benedicat!*

ONE pleasant afternoon in June, forty-eight years
ago, my father came to a window of his ancient
mansion-house, where my mother was seated, and
smilingly said to her, —

" This is a delightful day."

" Yes," she replied, " June is indeed the king of
months."

They happily continued their conversation for
half an hour, I, meanwhile, listening to what they
said.   They told one another little incidents relating to their parents.   Their happy smiles during
this interview were as pleasant as the sunny day to
which allusion was made.

NOTE. — *The setting of the types, and the press-work or printing of
this book, were performed by its author, principally evenings, after doing
his regular day's work of ten hours.*